The MIST and the FLAME

CORAL-LI ST. HELEN

CANTRAIP
PRESS

Cantraip Press
2317 Saratoga Place
Charleston, IL 61920
www.cantraippress.com

Publisher's Note: This is a work of fiction. Names, characters, places, and incidents are a product of the author's imagination. The works of Shakespeare are used imaginatively.

Book interior and cover by Damonza.com
Author photo by Aldo Manfroi
The Mist and the Flame / Coral-Li St. Helen
Paperback ISBN 978-1-942737-37-7
Electronic ISBN 978-1-942737-38-4

In memory of my mother

PART I

Lumi

"SO, DEAR COUSIN, are you excited for tonight?" Juliet turned from her overstuffed wardrobe of glittering gowns and gave me an arch smile. "I dare not answer. You will mock me no matter what I say."

"Will I? I wasn't aware I had such a reputation for mockery," I said, my eyes comically wide with feigned innocence.

"You *know* you do, Rosaline. If I say 'yes' you will laugh at me for being excited about something so silly, and if I say 'no'—" She broke off and hastily held up a blood-red velvet dress that dazzled with gold brocade, tilting her head as if considering its merits, though I doubted she even perceived what color it was. Her eyes had a faraway look, and despite the lightness of her tone, there was a melancholy air about her.

"*If* you say no? Would you?"

She pretended (because I knew it was pretense) to fuss over the other items before her. There seemed an endless number of them, all of the finest quality and highest fashion—my aunt Capulet's doing, no doubt. She could tell you down to the tiniest satin ribbon what the good ladies of Venice and Milan would be wearing even before they knew it themselves—and could afford to dress herself and her daughter accordingly, despite Juliet's lack of enthusiasm for these crucial matters.

Any other girl about to be presented at her first family banquet would have indulged in everything that her vanity craved. And hers was not just any ordinary family; these were the Capulets, one of the great families of Verona. Then again, Juliet was not just any ordinary girl.

Nor was I, for that matter. This, after all, was not to be my first but rather my last appearance at this kind of event.

"They want me to marry," Juliet said abruptly.

"Of course they do," I replied, and waited a moment for her to continue.

"They want me to marry Count Paris."

"And? How do you feel about the gallant young man? Yes, all right, I see what you mean; that sounded like mockery," I added, softening. I could see she was brooding over something, and I had a feeling I knew what it was. "Do you object?"

"No," she said, but she stretched out the word like a wistful note in a sad song.

"I will ask again, Cousin, with no mockery whatsoever: how do you feel about Count Paris?"

"I don't," she blurted. The delicate silk sash she had been fingering was now flung away as if it were a serpent. "I don't feel anything about him. I don't *know* him."

"Ah, stop there," I interrupted. "It's not that you don't know him. Don't say that, for you know what the response will be: 'You'll have plenty of time to get to know him after you are married.'" My cousin's weary sigh told me I was right and she'd heard this too many times already. "And what's more, you won't know the person you *do* fall in love with, not at all. That will be part of the reason you fall. Who doesn't love a good mystery?"

Her delicate brows knitted together. "I know nothing about Paris and I feel nothing for Paris! And I'm supposed to *marry* him—to entwine the rest of my life with his?"

"It's not just that you feel nothing for him, Juliet. You are being *told* what to feel about him, and that is impossible."

Now Juliet's eyes flashed astonishment, like two newly made stars. "Yes! That is it exactly. How can one love on command?"

"One does not. There is only one thing a person can do on command: obey. All else is irrelevant, at least to the one commanding."

She waited eagerly, as though for some additional bit of wisdom I could bestow upon her that would somehow give her the answer to all her problems. I tried not to laugh, as that most certainly would come across as disdain. Since my announcement that I would be going to the convent at La Fortezza by the end of June, people treated me in one of only two ways: as the object of pity or else as a great sage, wise beyond her years.

"You'll have to cut your lovely hair off, you know," the first type always said. Then, "Ah, the poor hearts you'll break if you do." *If.* As though these stupid things they said would change my mind. As though the effect my decision had on others was the only thing that mattered, and not the effect it would have on *me*, on *my* life.

The other type, the seeker of sage wisdom, was rarer, but also more difficult to deal with. There she was, my lovely cousin, looking at me with forlorn longing, face open like a flower, waiting for answers. Whatever made her think I had any? I wasn't interested in anything so dull as simple answers anyway; I wanted more than that.

I wanted... the world! And nothing less. Juliet was not the first person to accuse me of mockery, of being disdainful, even haughty—"You behave," my mother had said on more than one occasion, "as though everyone around you is lacking in something that only you have. It is not a pleasing look, Rosaline." Well, I could not help my demeanor when it truly reflected my feelings. Sometimes I looked around me at the all-too-familiar people and scenes—men itching for a fight, women anxious for their beauty to be noticed—and felt a volcanic rage building up. Didn't anyone else want *more* than that? Didn't they want to see the world through new eyes? I certainly did. There were so many amazing places beyond Verona, beyond even Italy. This fourteenth century of our Lord, people were saying proudly, was a golden age: magnificent works of art and architecture, great books full of ideas, glorious gardens to stroll through, enchanting music to hear, and so much more I had only heard about but wanted to experience for myself. And now I knew a way to get at least a little of it—and maybe a lot more—though I could not tell this to anyone else. I let them think I was giving up the world, instead of taking it on. That, they would accept; it allowed them to feel superior.

It pained me to think of Juliet and so many other girls like her who were missing this golden age, having nothing but the slim chance of personal romantic love to hope for. And they were the lucky ones; they didn't have to worry daily about how they would feed the ever-increasing brood that resulted from such love. Why should I be one of them, given the chance to do otherwise; why should I be relegated to being only a wife, and then a mother, and nothing else? I most certainly mocked *that* idea.

But in the meantime, Juliet the open-faced flower awaited my decrees. "Jule, dear," I sighed. "This is what your life will be from now on. A child does what it's told unquestioningly, or it does not and is punished. You're not a child anymore, and that makes things more complicated. If you do what you're told against your own desires, you'll be resentful and bitter. If you don't do what you're told, a simple punishment won't be the only consequence."

We both gazed out the chamber's window into the verdant gardens below—and then, unavoidably, at the imposing stone wall just beyond the charming flower beds and sparkling fountains. It was warm and sunny, as only a day in early summer can be in Verona, but the wall seemed to cast a chilly shadow over everything. I continued quietly, "You know that if you refuse Paris, your father will be disappointed, probably even angry. But beyond that, you are unable to perceive just yet. You do not know if you'll regret your refusal. *That* is the worst of it."

Juliet moved slowly away from the window, eyes downcast, as if it didn't really matter what was outside. In some way, I reflected sadly, it didn't matter to her; the stone wall marked the limits of her existence. She would be protected against harm—and safe from having any new experiences. "Yes—well, perhaps," she said, sighing. "Oh, Rosaline, laugh at me if you want but I want to *love* my husband."

A gloomy silence fell upon that normally light, airy room, and I knew we were both thinking of our own parents' marriages. Neither my mother nor hers had any affection for her husband, the evidence of which we saw continuously. It was hard to decide which was worse: my parents had once been in love, for a wild heartbeat or two; hers never had been, their marriage arranged much as Juliet's was now being orchestrated.

My aunt, Lady Capulet, might have been the only person who seemed at times to envy me, if in a resentful way. After all, I was escaping *her* fate.

The end result was the same for each married couple: they tolerated each other at best, with tolerance darkening frequently into loathing. Was it worse when something that started so splendidly ended up fading so quickly and completely—or to be entirely deprived of such splendor?

That question was irrelevant to my cousin. Her fate had already been decided. "You want a love marriage," I said quietly. "Why would I laugh at that? Do you not imagine every girl on the threshold of that life wouldn't think the same?"

"*You* don't."

There was a flicker of uncertainty on her face, as if she wasn't sure she should have said that, but she continued defiantly, "You have made it clear, Rosaline, that you care not for love. Many men, I am sure, would marry you if you would have them, but you love none of them—you have no love for love itself."

I turned away to hide my frown. It was not meant for her; my displeasure was entirely for another. Never mind that he was a Montague and my family aligned with the Capulets and the two families were sworn enemies. Never mind that I repeatedly, firmly, in ways that could not possibly be mistaken for coyness or flirtation or anything but honesty, refused him. For at least a fortnight, Romeo Montague had been swearing his undying love every chance he got. He said that love was for me, but I knew otherwise: Romeo was in love with love, and he could hardly have picked a worse person as the object of his amorousness. As Juliet said, I had no love for love, and definitely none for Romeo. Yet somehow this only fueled his feelings all the more.

It began, as all things do in this town, because of a fight. Capulets and Montagues, battling for their honor in the streets near my family's house, men young and old rushing into the fray, all except for one, I noticed from the safety of an upstairs room, one boy who hung back. Not out of cowardice, I surmised, for several of his friends had been shielding him such that he couldn't have thrown himself into the battle if he tried. I knew immediately that this must be Lord Montague's son. The look on his face—weariness mixed with restlessness, if that makes any sense—expressed exactly my own feelings at that moment. Fighting, again—what a complete waste of time, of energy, of life itself! I shook my head involuntarily, and the motion must have caught his attention, for we locked eyes and stared at each other. Then he bowed his head in acknowledgement, and I knew he understood. I nodded, and turned away from the window.

It was a nice moment, and that should have been the end of it, but of course it wasn't, not with Romeo. He might not have had any interest in the blood feud, to his credit, but he seemed to have substituted one kind of mad obsession with another. He pursued me, declared his undying love every chance he got to everyone he knew; I avoided him and told no one. Luckily our social circles did not overlap beyond perhaps our priest, Friar Lawrence, whose discretion was absolute.

Thus Juliet did not know about Romeo's affections for me—she did not know Romeo Montague at all beyond his name, never having met him—and most likely she would never know, since I strongly suspected the young man would eagerly give his heart to another (with any luck, more suitable) once I was gone and the whole thing would be forgotten. I turned back to my cousin, masking my vexation with a teasing smile.

"'You have no love for love.' Such a proclamation! You don't need my guidance, Cos. You know the ways of the world so well already."

"I do *not* know—I do not understand. How can you be so sure of what you want? You are scarcely twelve months my senior."

"I am well over a year your senior, and a lot can happen between the ages of thirteen and fifteen. And how can you be sure yourself? *Love*, you declare, but what does that even mean to you?"

To my surprise, she spun around and waved her arms as if in an ecstatic dance. "It means everything. It means—magic."

She looked so full of life and longing, this time I laughed at her with delight. "Magic. Oh Juliet, there's magic everywhere, not just in handsome young men."

My answer surprised her. She stopped her twirling and stared at me. "Everywhere? Even where you're going?"

I knew I shouldn't have said it, but I did anyway: "Especially where I'm going."

Juliet looked quizzical but didn't ask what I meant; I suspect she put my remark down as yet another peculiar utterance by her odd cousin.

This was lucky, I reflected a few minutes later when I left her to prepare for the evening's festivities in my guest's room. As I watched the servants scampering up and down the grand staircase and across the long halls, I smiled to myself. I had a secret, one that I'd almost revealed to my cousin. How surprised she would have been—how surprised would they all be! I pictured everyone suddenly stopping in their tracks, dropping what they carried, staring at me. The thought made me giggle. A servant, struggling with a large bronze ewer as though it were a prize he regretted having won, glanced at me but hurried on. All this, and I cared nothing for any of it; I would leave it all behind tomorrow morning.

"Why," they all asked. "Why would you give up your home, your family, your lovely hair?" (What was so special about hair, anyway? People did realize it grew back, didn't they?) "What if you change your mind?" (What if I don't? People always believed they knew better than I did what I would want. How could that *possibly* be?)

What was so special about La Fortezza?

What was so special was this: *magic*. Real magic, not the kind that was all self-delusion. What was magical about love? If you loved a person who did not love you, no magic would ever change that; you simply turned your gaze to someone else, until you found someone who happened to be looking at you the same way.

And that thought ended up giving me the worst idea I've ever had.

But getting to that terrible decision required a bit of a journey, one that began with an assignment from my Latin tutor, of all things and all people. This young man was possibly the least magical person I'd ever met. His presence in a room was like that one heavy cloud that insists on dimming the sun on an otherwise fine day. He was probably no more than five years older than I was, but he seemed ancient, not in the way of old people or things that are grand and stately but in his very lifelessness. His clothing was always drab, his voice never varied in pitch or tone; even his tight, thin smile, the very few times he displayed one, made you feel glum. He could make even the most interesting subjects seem deadly dull, which is precisely why, I believe, he was so frequently employed by wealthy families with daughters. There was no danger that they would form an undesirable attachment to him, and little chance they would enjoy their studies to the point of becoming unbecomingly scholarly. So twice a week he bored my younger sister and me with instruction in Greek and Latin, during which time my sister Livia found ways to nap discreetly behind a large book and I stared at the wall above the man's head, daydreaming of all things magical—really, all things other than what was happening in the room at the moment.

Magic as an area of study was not shocking by itself in these enlightened times—far from it. Our own friar's use of various flowers, leaves, seeds, and roots for medicine was considered magic, after all, and it was accepted by everyone who knew him. It was different for women and girls, though. I was aware that there were women with expertise in this kind of medicine, but they kept it a secret known only to a very few, and their purview was entirely women's matters: how to have a baby, how not to have a baby, and a few other things I'd heard whispered about but abruptly cut short once my presence was known. And for girls, even from good families, studying anything with zeal simply did not happen. To be appropriately accomplished, they might excel in one area such as music, but their excellence could only manifest itself in performance for others, not for their own gratification, and certainly not for their own glory.

On the particular day that started it all, our tutor, Grigio, gave me something to translate which turned out to be an old recipe for a potion to be used for suppressing painful memories. It called for various common herbs which I knew Friar Lawrence grew in his garden, so I ran to him the first chance I got to ask for the ingredients. That, I found out later, was how the school at La Fortezza became interested in me. Friar Lawrence and, incredibly, my tutor both looked out for potential candidates to recruit for this secret school. Most of the tutor's pupils, my cousin Juliet included, merely did the translation (perfectly, in her case). The very few with the curiosity to see if it would work, those were the ones that interested them.

But I knew none of that at the time; I was only interested in making the potion work. Initially, it didn't, and I figured out there had been an ingredient omitted—possibly deliberately, so Grigio's students wouldn't have the complete formula. That was laughable—and insulting. I immediately began experimenting on my own, trying to figure out the missing item. (This extra step, apparently, made La Fortezza *very* interested in me.) My creations, placed discretely in various rooms, made me sneeze (not magical), made the cook giggle (possibly magical, since she generally had a dour disposition), and made my parents look at each other in a way I hadn't seen in years (which was uncomfortable to witness but also possibly magical). I noted these combinations of ingredients down and, not satisfied, kept trying.

When I couldn't quite come up with the perfect formula on my own, I sought the friar again. If Grigio was a young man who seemed like an old one, Friar Lawrence was, if not old, then middle-aged at least, but cheerful, jovial, and youthful in every aspect of his demeanor. To put it another way, he was possibly the only priest that people my age actually liked, someone who talked to you like a person and not just a sinner. In his little garden behind the church he welcomed me with delight, a dirt-crusted trowel in one hand and some mysterious wrinkled root in the other, immediately asking how my potion had gone.

"Not well, thank you. It didn't work, but I think I know how I can fix it—with your help, if you would."

"I would be most delighted to help," he said, eager curiosity shining in his eyes. He put down the trowel and root, dusted his cassock off (though his hands were dirty too and he really only ended up shifting the soiling of the garment to different sections), and gestured me toward a bench where we both sat. "Now, how did you know it didn't work?"

"I tried. A *lot*. The closest I got was when I tried it on Bruno, but even then it still wasn't right."

"Bruno?"

"The old dog I found wandering around outside our gate. I named him Bruno. Poor thing. He had been treated very badly, we think by a man or several of them—he is afraid of men. I wanted to see if I could help him forget his suffering. He seemed to be calmer when I sprinkled one particular herbal powder mix around him, but he still growls and shrinks away when a man goes by, so he hasn't completely forgotten."

The friar smiled. "That was kind of you to try, though a human subject might have been more able to communicate what they were experiencing."

I shrugged. I wanted to try it on the dog because I wanted to alleviate his suffering. His big brown eyes were deep with sorrow. How could I do otherwise? I went on impatiently, "I know why it didn't work—there's an ingredient missing, isn't there?"

Friar Lawrence tilted his head. "Yes and no. Well, yes and yes, I suppose. The recipe as you received it is in fact missing an ingredient, but that ingredient alone—stridolo petals, I believe—will not make this work. The real missing ingredient is *you*. Bruno calmed down because you were calm. Bruno cannot forget whatever suffering he went through, no matter what herbs you use, because you can't forget it—because you never remembered it in the first place."

"Of course not. I wasn't there." Now I frowned. Did I, too, have to be beaten and starved by cruel men for both of us to forget? Wasn't there an easier way to help my poor sad-eyed friend? There was a limit to what even I wished to experience. "How can I make these things work without, well, going through terrible things?"

"It is a long and difficult journey to take, Rosaline. But I can try to show you the first steps." He shifted a little on the bench so that he was facing me. "Think of a happy memory from your childhood, but don't tell me about it."

His simple request startled me. Was he going to *read my mind*? If so, I figured I should pick something very obscure and detailed, something he couldn't possibly guess, but the first thing that came to my mind was small and simple, and once there refused to leave. Seconds later, the friar exclaimed, "Ah, amaretti! I love those delicious little cookies. They say Venice has the best, but I think our Veronese version quite superior, don't you?"

I stared at him, alarmed, stammering stupidly, "How did you... that's... you know my thoughts!"

He shook his head vigorously. "Oh no, Rosaline, no. I recalled just that one memory, you and your sister eating almond cookies that your father had brought back from Venice." He chuckled. "It seems you were especially pleased because he rarely brought back treats, and because there were an odd number and you, the elder, got the extra. But what I did just now is the absolute limit of my abilities in this area. I could never tell you everything you are thinking and feeling at any given moment; no one can do that. Magic doesn't work like that."

I desperately wanted to know how it *did* work, but he was continuing to speak. "Now you try. You suggest something for me to think of."

"And then what?"

"Hear yourself asking the question as though you were me. Smell the scent of these herbs." I had not even noticed the small bouquet of dried leaves and twigs he had drawn from his pocket and placed on the bench beside us, but I must have been sensing their aroma all along. "Think of how we'll both be experiencing the same thing at that moment in terms of our senses. Imagine that you're *me*, breathing in the aroma. Live this moment as though you were me. Then see what comes to you."

I felt jittery with excitement but calmed myself with a deep breath. The herbs smelled of pine forests, damp earth, cool breezes, and, incongruously, smoke. I studied the friar's genial expression and then, quietly, said, "Think of the last person who made you angry."

The friar closed his eyes for a moment and then opened them, keeping his expression the same. I could have sworn there was a glint in his eye, though, especially when I knew the answer.

"That was too easy!" I laughed. "It's the same person for me!"

Friar Lawrence grinned. "The fact that we were both last angered by the same person—and likely for the same reason— does not take away from your success, though he *is* a trying youth these days. Still, you would never have guessed it was Romeo; you found him in my memories."

And found it shockingly easy to do so, I thought. My mind whirled with questions. "I'm no one special," I forced myself to say, though privately I didn't believe it. "And I could do this immediately. Can *anyone* do this kind of magic?"

"Again, yes and no. Most people could do a little if they tried, but unless they are given guidance, they would never *know* to try it." He found a small bowl of ripe berries on a work table hidden among gardening tools, books, cut branches, and piles of leaves and offered the fruit to me. "All children throw things. Toys, food, dirt. That motion comes naturally. But that doesn't mean they will all grow up to be expert spear-throwers—unless they train specifically for it. Likewise, many people possess certain abilities that come naturally—that aren't considered magic, but—"

"But they could become that," I said breathlessly. "Like how people sometimes know what another person is thinking, but it isn't magic, just perceptiveness."

"Correct. And like anything else, gaining expertise in magic is greatly aided by expert instruction. To use a better analogy, it's like learning a language—like Latin. Some people are a lot better at it than others, and no one at all is born knowing it, but nearly everyone has the potential to learn it and nearly everyone can benefit from outside guidance."

I did not want to hear about Latin anymore. "So, that magic we did. Can a person *prevent* you from seeing their memories? Even a person who doesn't know magic?"

"Of course. I think I may have made this look far too simple, my child. Remember, we know each other, we told each other what to think about, and we were both willing participants, plus we had the herbs I'd chosen, which aren't necessary but definitely help. It's a different matter entirely with a stranger who could be thinking anything at all—or hiding what they really think. That is where magic comes in—and a lot of practice."

"What about... can it work the other way?" I asked with trepidation. "Can you make someone remember something that never happened? Or experience something that isn't happening? That would be extremely dangerous," I added hastily, in case he thought this was something I planned on doing. It wasn't; I had too many other ideas I wanted to try.

"It can be done, but it almost never *is* done—not even by those who use magic for ill gain. The one perpetrating the spell is just as much in danger of believing the false memories or experiences as the victim, so nothing would be gained. But if you can see the present, the real present—put yourself in a person's point of view, enter their mind at the current moment, and from there—"

He broke off abruptly. "But this is not my area of expertise, Rosaline. I focus on remedies from plants—'beneficial botany,' I call it. For you to expand your understanding, you would need to go to the school at La Fortezza and study."

"How do I do that?" I demanded to know, before I had even the slightest idea what the school at La Fortezza might be.

And that was how it began—how I ended up about to embark on the greatest adventure I could possibly imagine.

La Fortezza was not far from Verona, but it might as well have been nestled among the stars, it seemed so strange and far away. It was ancient—Roman Empire-ancient, the friar told me. Its inhabitants studied what we would call magic, though they didn't officially call it that—"provecta scientia," the friar believed was the terminology used back then, "and their credo is 'tantum facere bonum,' or 'only do good,' which you didn't ask about but I thought I'd mention anyway." It wasn't an ordinary convent even if it superficially seemed like one: the austere name and secluded location, the shapeless cloaks the nuns wore, their terse replies or even complete silence if anyone encountered them in town bringing fruit or honey to the market to sell. It was a place to study magic. Most of the nuns studied botanical magic, like he did, since they farmed the land, but the secret school, as it was called, went much further than that. "And to know more, you will need to travel there yourself. If you're willing, there's a place for you."

Willing? I had been ready to go right then and there. And now it was happening at last.

The morning I left for La Fortezza was the happiest moment of my life up to that point. I couldn't wait to get there. My family set out a grand breakfast in my honor: fresh bread, fine cheese, roasts and sausages, and beautiful pyramids of the sweetest fruits of the season. I am sure this was not so much to give me something to enjoy as it was to remind me what I would be missing from now on. I could not reveal the truth to them, so they naturally figured I would be surviving on stale crusts and murky water. I thanked them graciously, helped myself to an overripe fig, and smiled as I chewed its bland mush, thinking about how much of this bounty actually came from the land around La Fortezza—and this wasn't even the best of it. That was for the inhabitants, who helped with the farming. They had to eat, too, and it couldn't be helped that what they ate was abundant and fresh.

Upon my final departure, I barely said three words to my mother and father and sister (three words in total, one apiece), and they said even fewer to me. I got more affection from dear old Bruno, who licked my hand when I scratched his furry chin. It was not that I wanted to get away from them so badly; I just very badly wanted to get to La Fortezza. My family was not nearly as well off as the Capulets—few families were—but we certainly had enough of everything necessary for a comfortable life. My parents' rules were mostly reasonable, punishments on the lenient side, affection given sparingly but sincerely. I had nothing to complain about—and nothing to hope for because of it. Each day would promise the drab sameness of the one before, each hour of that day would fall like a hammer, rhythmically pounding out any protest I might have, anything stubbornly different about me. And this would continue, I knew, for the rest of my life, unless I got out.

As for my parents, they were not angry with me either, just puzzled and a little disappointed that I'd chosen the life of a nun. They had never believed me particularly pious (I wasn't), and they thought I was pretty enough to make a good match (I didn't care). Well, they would have to wait a few years and pin their hopes on Livia, who was just as pretty and even less pious than they perceived me to be, as she frequently had to be dragged out of bed, yawning and rubbing her eyes theatrically, to attend mass. She was also a practical girl who didn't believe in magic, or at least didn't give it any thought, being far more interested in what she might eat at our next meal and how she might get larger portions now that I was leaving.

La Fortezza was only about an hour by carriage outside the edge of the city, but it was farther than I'd ever been, and each clop of the horse's hooves made my heart boom in tandem. I hardly took in any of the scenery, though, until my father's carriage stopped and I was let out.

I knew the fortress was the remnants of Roman ruins, but despite its name and history, it looked less imposing than it did intriguing. The actual buildings were all contemporary and ordinary; it was only the wall running around the perimeter that made use of the ancient stone edifice. Even here, the ruins had been augmented with other, newer, materials—wood, brick, wrought iron for the gate—with no attempt at unity or order. And yet the finished wall appeared oddly seamless—and even natural, somehow. Looking at the wall was like looking at time itself.

A nun stood at the main gate to meet me. A real nun, in a nun's drab cloak, which startled me even though it shouldn't have. There was a real convent at La Fortezza, of course, but once I'd heard about the magic part of it I figured the convent was just a convenient disguise for its true purpose. For a horrifying moment I was afraid there had been a misunderstanding and they believed I was really there to be a nun.

As if sensing this, she smiled reassuringly. "I am here to take you to your room, Rosaline." Her voice was deeper than I'd expected, and she was fairly tall, and I wondered about rumors I'd heard that some of the nuns at La Fortezza were actually men seeking sanctuary. That seemed odd to me—wouldn't they just be sent to a monastery?—plus the rumored male nuns were purported to be castrati, who wouldn't have deep voices anyway, if they existed at all. Perhaps such men found La Fortezza more welcoming than anywhere else. Perhaps they felt they could belong here—*did*, in fact, belong here. I was too excited by all the newness around me to pursue that line of thought, though, as the nun continued, "I call you that name for possibly the last time, by the way—you may choose your own name."

"Anything I want?" I asked eagerly.

This engendered a warm smile. "Of course. It is *your* name. For example, I call myself Corridore Veloce, or just Corri, because when I was a child my favorite thing was to run as fast as I could until I collapsed." A giggle slipped out of me, and Corri smiled again. "I am too old for that now, alas, but I do frequently take La Fortezza's carriage into town for errands, and sometimes I drive the horses faster than I should. Not until they collapse, of course, dear things, but until we are all quite happy to be alive on God's great earth."

I felt happiness to be alive bubbling up in me at that moment, too. I liked Corri—were they all like this here? I glanced toward the main buildings, impatient to meet the others. Who would they be, these other students of magic? What names had they chosen for themselves? And what name would I choose for myself? I could make something up that was purely new. No saints and martyrs *here*. I restrained myself from skipping a gleeful circle around my guide.

We turned from the gate and Corri led me just a short way toward a cluster of small huts, clean and attractive with small beds of flowers surrounding each one. There were rows of herbs and vegetables between here and the main buildings. Fruit trees lined one side of the fields, and the hum of bees suggested the famous La Fortezza apiary wasn't far off. The huts all seemed to be deserted though, and I looked longingly at the main buildings again, which seemed disappointingly far away. I supposed I would have to wait to meet the others.

Corri cleared her throat to regain my attention, and I was shown to a hut. "This is your room. You'll find everything you need here. When you are ready, Syra will come here to see you."

I almost blurted out a foolish question about how this Syra would know I was ready but luckily did not, merely nodded. Of course she would know—she was probably the head of the school and an expert in all things magical.

Inside the hut was a cozy dwelling, certainly not opulent but also not as austere as most people seemed to imagine a convent's living quarters. To be honest, I had imagined them that way, too, and a sigh of relief escaped me. While it didn't feel like home just yet, I thought I could get used to this space. A small table with two chairs, a bed with clean linens, a washstand with a pitcher and bowl, and a glass—that was pretty much it. I stared at my reflection in the glass for a moment and then impulsively dug into the bag containing my few possessions and brought out a pair of sewing scissors. I had no idea if I was even required to cut my hair—La Fortezza seemed to do things differently from other convents after all—but I didn't care. This felt like something I needed to do. I pulled off my cap and pins, grabbed my hair in one hand, shoved it into the V of the open scissors, and cut.

It took but seconds. I looked in the glass and gazed at my image. My face looked so—exposed. My eyes seemed huge, like an owl's. I lidded them partway, but then I just looked like a furtive owl. My skin had a sallow tinge—was this how I truly looked and I'd never noticed until now? Was this really *me*? I could actually see the nervous perspiration on my forehead. What had I done?

Then I looked down and burst out laughing. The hair looked so ridiculous clutched in my fist, dead brown strands that Romeo and a few other silly youths had all but worshiped. How did they like my shimmering tresses now? Everything from my old life seemed ridiculous, for that was what I called it, my "old life," even though I'd only left it a short while ago. This was my new life, with a different look, even a different name. I had already picked mine out: Foschia Luminosa. Bright Mist. I liked the way it sounded, both mysterious and powerful at once. And—yes, I *did* like the way I looked. I felt strangely calmed by my own appearance at that moment, an odd thing to feel after all that frenetic excitement. There was a just-rightness about it that I'd never experienced until now.

Remembering that Syra would be here soon, I hastily put the hair away in a drawer—there were many uses for cut hair, so my frugal mother had once told me, including stuffing cushions, which ruined my sleep for weeks—and sat at the table to wait. As if she'd been standing right outside the door waiting for me to do just that, Syra entered.

And Syra was… scary. Possibly the most terrifying person I've ever encountered, and I could not for the life of me figure out why. There was nothing unusual about her appearance, other than an ageless quality—she wasn't young anymore, clearly, but she could be anywhere from my mother's age to well beyond my grandmother's. She wore the same kind of shapeless gray cloak as Corri had. At one moment her complexion seemed as fair as sun-bleached bone and the next, as she turned her face just slightly to the side, dark as the unlit corners of a room. She was neither small nor large, tall nor short. But her presence in that room seemed to hush all sounds, freeze all movements, almost stopped my breathing. When she walked toward me, it felt more like I was being pulled toward her; with her eyes on mine, I felt stripped bare—not just of clothes but of my skin and flesh, as if she were observing the ever-faster beating of my heart.

She sat at the table opposite me, and the first words said to me were these: "You have done wrong." Her voice was quiet, her accent not Veronese but from I knew not where, and I felt each syllable in my bones as if she'd roared like a lion.

And I regret to say I knew immediately what she meant.

All I did was turn his gaze from me to her. I had been thinking about the conversation I had with my cousin, her yearning for love, for someone to look at the way he looked at me, and for him to see her the same way, so I gave her that. I gave him that as well, because even if he exasperated me with his persistence, he deserved a chance to get what he desired. So when I noticed that Romeo and some of his Montague brethren had snuck into the Capulet banquet, I put my newly discovered powers of magic to use.

I had been pondering what the friar had said about "seeing the present." I had the sense that if you could put yourself in another's point of view—sharing their perceptions and sensations—you might be able to influence their actions. Not in any excessive way, not in a way that might cause harm, but in small ways, and it wouldn't even require concoctions of herbs, since the friar had suggested those were mainly for getting the magicker's mind in the right frame and not so much for influencing the subject. It was certainly worth trying, I figured. I'd always wanted to perceive the world through other eyes.

I envisioned myself seeing the room as Romeo was seeing it at that moment—the glittering lights, the weaving bodies of dancers—and then envisioned turning just a little farther left, past the dancers and toward the back of the room, and seeing... her. Juliet. Radiant as the sun, she made everything else disappear before his eyes, including, to my delight, me. He stepped closer, and the movement caught her attention. She turned her eyes to him.

It had worked. I knew it wasn't just coincidence; I had felt it happen, felt our minds lock together and my mind moving him.

"I thought it would be all right," I said softly, trying to

control the trembling in my voice. "I thought everyone would get something they wanted—myself included," I added for honesty's sake.

But Syra would not be fooled. "You did not do that for them. You did it entirely for you. And you have no idea what will follow. You think they will fall in love and be happy? Part of that is correct, yes. But partial truth is no better than no truth at all."

I could not speak, and clearly I was not supposed to. Syra's stern face prohibited me almost from breathing. "Romeo and Juliet fall in love, yes. And it will be their ruin."

I wanted to ask how she knew this, not because I didn't believe her but because I very much wanted to learn it too. I had a feeling that would not have helped my case at all.

"You want to know how I know this," Syra said. I nodded dumbly—what else could I do? "I will help you understand. First, however, let us see what your actions prevented."

From under the table she produced a small earthen bowl (where had *that* come from?), which she placed before me. I expected herbs, leaves, and flowers, as Friar Lawrence had used, but the bowl's contents looked more like sand, and I could not discern any particular odor.

Suddenly the memory of the banquet burst into my mind. I was in the Capulets' grand ballroom. On one side of the musicians, Juliet stood with her mother; on the other side, poorly disguised and craning his neck looking for me, Romeo. This time, I did not avert Romeo's gaze to Juliet. I did nothing, and they never saw each other that night. They never met.

The memory faded, then continued, though it wasn't a memory anymore but... what was it? A memory of the *future*? A vision, perhaps? In any case, dimly but with no uncertainty,

I saw Juliet marry Paris. That was no surprise to me; everyone knew she would, despite what she had confided to me, despite my uncle's claim that it would be "her own decision." Yes, her decision as long as it conceded to his will, that was my uncle all over. Also not surprising, my cousin was a beautiful bride, Paris a handsome groom, the wedding lavish as only a Capulet affair could be. The couple did not smile much, but it was not considered proper (or fashionable, my aunt would no doubt assert) to smile at a wedding, especially not for the demure, chaste bride. That, I reflected wryly, was convenient. No one would know how she really felt, whether she loved or loathed the man by her side, whether she dreaded or desired her first night with him.

And afterward? The vision blurred into fog, but impressions continued to flow through my mind. Was it a marriage, as she and I both abhorred, like her parents'? At first, I sensed that yes, it was. But Paris was not like my uncle in certain key ways; he had not my uncle Capulet's fiery temper, nor his overbearing ego. Were they happy? He certainly was. And Juliet—well, I had a hard time discerning that. I doubt she had that grand passion she dearly desired. But was that so very bad?

Before I could see my cousin's situation with any more clarity, the vision ended. "And now," said Syra crisply—how had she known it was over?—"I will help you to find out what happens instead. You know both the young lady and the young gentleman, so it is within your power to envision their future. Place yourself back at the moment of their meeting and envision their future."

She had said *envision* rather than *imagine*, though I did not see what the difference was. Still, if it was within my power, I would "envision" a happy outcome. I did as she instructed and let the vision come.

I saw them in a dark place, lying together in each other's arms. It was not romantic; it was ghastly. The air was cold, dank, smelling of decay. Their limbs were rigid, their faces stiff and still. Foam had bubbled from Romeo's lips, suggesting poison, and indeed a small empty vial lay next to one pale hand. Juliet lay next to him with her arms around his lifeless form, a dagger deep in her chest and her blood blanketing them both. Their eyes stared, unseeing, hard as stones, into mine.

I shrieked, jolting back into the present moment, gasping as if I'd run a very long way. And I did desperately want to run away from what I'd seen.

Syra was silent for several minutes, letting me calm myself, before speaking again. "Even if this were not the case, even if this horrific outcome were not a given, what is the first rule of La Fortezza?"

"Only do good," I replied promptly, though barely in a whisper.

"Yes. Do not ever mean harm, and do not merely mean to do good: do good itself, always. And you did not. Selfish actions are never only good, no matter how we might wish to justify them. In this case, you have done considerable harm in your selfish act. In order to enter La Fortezza, you must right that wrong. What you have seen is a possible future; you must prevent what you have just seen from coming true."

"How?" I gasped. "I barely know how to do any of—this," I gestured vaguely around me. "Magic," I added, in case she hadn't understood.

Which was stupid—of course she understood. Syra smiled very faintly. "Then this will be an excellent way to learn."

So it was that I returned to Verona the same day I thought I had left it for good. I was cloaked and shorn of hair but otherwise no different. No, I *was* different—I was a hundred times more desperate and felt even less like I could do anything about it.

I had La Fortezza's carriage, driven by a sympathetic but silent Corri, take me to see Friar Lawrence, since it was the only place I could think to go. If I'd absorbed little of the view on my way from Verona because of my excitement, I saw none of it at all on my way back. The carriage was surprisingly opulent, the ride much smoother than it had been in my father's carriage, but they might as well have flung me in the back of a farmer's rickety cart or slung me over a donkey like a sack of flour. It was as much as I deserved for making such a mess of things so quickly.

I trudged back into the little garden behind the church where once again Friar Lawrence stood bent over his herbs, muttering to himself in his quietly jolly way. When he looked up to see me, before he had time to show his shock, I blurted, "I failed."

He wasn't shocked, just a little confused. "As do we all, when we are learning something new. I don't understand, child—please explain."

I explained, briefly. I had tried some magic on my own, involving my cousin and Romeo. I had succeeded. The results, I was shown by Syra, would be disastrous, so I was back to fix it, I knew not how. "I'm sorry, Friar Lawrence," I added miserably when he looked away with a furrowed brow.

"Oh no, my child, I'm not upset with you. I'm just surprised. This seems—unusual. Syra's making you come back like this, I mean." He shook his head, and I could have sworn he said her name as though he'd tasted something bitter.

"Did none of the others have to do this?" I asked anxiously. "Go back out and prove themselves?" Had I already distinguished myself, but in the worst possible way?

Now his frown disappeared entirely. "Rosaline, no 'others' have come from me. You are the first I have ever sent. No one else I've observed has shown your ability and drive."

At any other time I might have preened like a peacock at his praise, but in my distress I hardly registered it. His words didn't change the fact that here I was, nor the awful reason why. "Well, maybe no one else has failed so swiftly either. Regardless, I ask your help, Friar."

"And I willingly provide it, child. You needn't worry yourself; all will be well with your cousin and you will be back at La Fortezza in no time at all. I shall take care of the situation."

His words did not have the intended effect, for I felt more worried rather than less. "Friar, Syra told *me* to take care of it. If you do everything, how will that prove that I am worthy to study at the school?"

He considered me for a moment, and once again I had the sense that the name Syra displeased him. How could that be, when he had sent me to her to learn? Then he quickly smiled his usual cheery grin and exclaimed, "Very well! You can help by finding out what people are saying. I have some old servants' clothes in the vestry you can wear as a disguise. Go to the marketplace and listen in on conversations. Remember anything that might be useful. Be very careful; go there and back and don't linger."

I felt a stab of frustration; his task for me didn't sound like it would accomplish anything at all, which was perhaps what he intended. I had to *do* something, though; Syra had made that clear. I could not simply rely on the friar's intervention to solve everything. And La Fortezza was Syra's domain, not Friar Lawrence's. Whatever conflict there was between them was none of my business; I answered to Syra alone. I nodded and smiled at the friar, pretending to go along, all the while deciding a course of my own.

So off I went in a baggy woolen kirtle that had seen better days but was honestly the least restricting thing I'd ever worn. I chuckled to think of Romeo seeing me like this. He just might see me, at that; loathe as I was to see him again, I knew he would be easier to get alone than my cousin, though I had no idea what I'd say if I did manage that feat. It would be nearly impossible for me to get into the House of Capulet, no matter how well disguised, and to go as myself would require excuses and lies that would at best arouse considerable suspicion and at worst make them believe I ran away from the convent. They would return me to my parents' house, and I had no idea how I would explain any of this to them so that they would release me to return to La Fortezza—which I couldn't return to anyway, until I fixed everything.

Romeo, on the other hand, was at leisure to wander the streets and piazzas of Verona, as he was wont to do. It should not be difficult to find him and talk to him alone. That said, while my servant boy's disguise would allow me to roam the city alone in greater safety, I still had to be wary and not linger anywhere too long. Despite Prince Escalus's recent pronouncement of death to anyone who fought in the streets, there were still many roving groups of young men just itching to taunt and torment anyone they came across, and a lone boy was an easy target.

And yet this was the first time I had wandered, alone, the streets of the city in which I'd lived my whole life so far. I had heard it said that Verona was often dismissed as a merely adequate stopping point between the great cities of Venice and Milan. People who said this while in Verona were called fools by any citizen who happened to hear them. Yes, Venice was beautiful, Milan sophisticated, but Verona was quintessentially *Italian*, or so they insisted. I wouldn't have known, but I hoped to at least get out in it.

And then I *was* out in it. It was frightening. It was also exhilarating. I walked fast to keep from being stopped by anyone, and soon I was running, fast and free. I remembered what Corri had said about running as a child, and I burst into delighted laughter. Doorways passed in a blur, one after another; I saw little but didn't care. Dirt, stone, the occasional squish of horse droppings—all felt glorious beneath my feet. I wasn't sitting in a room in a house behind a wall; I was in the world at last. Part of me hoped I wouldn't find Romeo right away so I could just keep running.

I did find him, though, both too soon and too late. As I burst into the Piazza delle Erbe, I heard shouts, saw a mass of masculine bodies, and there he was, in the middle of the crowd facing Tybalt Capulet, just about the worst place Romeo Montague could be. There was blood on Tybalt's sword, rage on Romeo's face. Tybalt was generally regarded as the second-greatest swordsman in Verona.

The greatest, Mercutio, lay dead at their feet.

How was this possible? In a flash I realized that he must have died at Tybalt's hand. Mercutio's sightless eyes looked up toward the heavens, something like a half-smile on his lips. I stared at the corpse, feeling my own blood drain from my head, then shut my eyes. I had to clear my mind of this horror so that I could do what needed to be done—whatever that might be. Warily, I moved closer to the edge of the crowd.

My mother was Lady Capulet's sister; Tybalt, son of Lord Capulet's younger brother, was no blood kin of mine, and a rough brute in the bargain, thus I did not care whether he lived or died. Romeo I had to protect, as part of righting the wrong I had done. But there was no way this could be won. If by some miracle Romeo beat Tybalt, he would be executed given the prince's recent decree. But then perhaps Prince Escalus might show lenience, given that Mercutio was his kin and Romeo was clearly only avenging his dear friend's death. And if Tybalt were only wounded before the brawl was discovered, all the better.

So when I looked up and saw Romeo start to thrust his sword in what would have almost certainly been a death blow, I took action. I locked my mind with Romeo's again and deflected his sword just enough to the side.

Tybalt received little more than a scratch on his shoulder. The fight was broken up, the fighters were hustled away by their respective kinsmen to opposite corners of the piazza, and I exhaled for what felt like an hour.

It occurred to me, when I was able to breathe and think normally, that *this* was what magic was all about. It wasn't lightning bolts from fingertips; it wasn't even deception the way the street magicians did it, making you look at one thing while they were doing another. Really, it was very nearly the opposite: making yourself look at one thing and one thing only, shutting everything else out. In his mind, seeing what he saw, I had focused on Romeo's movements with the sword, and as the piazza, the crowds, the noises and movement all melted away, we, he and I, moved as one.

From Tybalt's corner came an eruption of shouting and wailing, interrupting my reverie. Men were screaming his name: "Tybalt! Tybalt!" Why? What was happening behind that wall of bodies? I craned my neck but saw nothing, and I was still too woozy—and wary—to move closer. Perhaps I could see what one of the bodies blocking my way could see? I tried it: I locked minds with one of the men in the crowd and I saw Tybalt—dead. There was no doubt of it. A great gash in his chest gushed blood where a dagger or sword had run through his heart.

My own heart felt like it would beat right out of my body. How was this possible? Romeo certainly had not done it. Could I make the man whose view I shared remember it? I tried, and it wasn't difficult (if nothing else, I certainly *was* doing as Syra had suggested and learning a lot of magic very quickly). Indeed, the man's memory showed someone else, swift as lightning, joining the crowd of Capulets around Tybalt and running the blade into him, in and out as fast as if it had merely been thrust in a pool of water to be cleansed. I could not see the face at all, but I did see one important thing: that person, the killer, was in red and gold. The colors of the House of Capulet.

No one else appeared to have seen that, though. Everyone was blaming Romeo. "Romeo must die," they chanted, and I knew I had failed again.

❧

In vain, I lingered in the piazza, desperately bouncing my mind from one person to another, trying to uncover any memory of having seen who had killed Tybalt. But there were so many of them, and they kept moving, and I had to keep moving as well lest I be accosted and questioned, that I couldn't focus, and nor could anyone else. The crowd around the corpse surged into a narrow alley, and I hesitated, not wanting to get trapped. Instead I turned and tried to run after Romeo and the Montagues, who had fled in the opposite direction. Here I met with no success either—they had vanished.

And then I realized I was lost. Unfamiliar structures loomed around me, blocking out the sunlight. The very air felt different, colder, damper, with strange murky smells. Was it still summer, and was this still Verona? But of course it was; this was yet more evidence of how little I knew the place I'd been born and raised. I whirled around and noticed there were no people here either, which was a relief at first until it became an additional cause for unease. There were no people I could *see*. There were plenty of shadowy spaces and darkened doorways where anything, anyone, might hide. There were sounds that could be whispers, or wind, or my imagination.

And then far to my left, almost but not quite out of my scope of vision, I saw a face. It was cast in shadow, but I *knew* it was a face—it could be nothing else—and it was looking directly at me.

I turned my head sharply toward it and it vanished, but it had been right *there*: a hard, malevolent face.

I turned my body even more sharply away from it and walked, fast, but not too fast, I hoped. *I should look confident, not scared.*

That tapping behind me—was it footsteps, or just a loose board swinging from an eave? I stopped again; the sound stopped.

And then started again, faster.

The sound was not coming any closer—yet my unease remained. It could still be a person, perhaps tapping the ground with one foot while watching me from the shadows, deliberately instigating my terror. I was frozen, my eyes darting around helplessly. The dark puddle to my left looked like blood, the dead leaf to my right appeared as a severed hand beckoning me forward.

I whirled around, hands on hips, a fierce scowl (I fervently wished) on my face. Something—someone—ducked back, but I saw the glint of metal before it disappeared into the shadows. The glint of a sword, a dagger, some sharp and vicious weapon.

If I kept going, it would be more of the same until I went mad with fear. If I approached the figure, unarmed as I was— well, that would be even worse. What could I do? Ridiculously I backed into a shallow recess in a stone wall and tried to make myself as small as possible. What good was my magic now? I was a young girl, poorly disguised, alone, vulnerable, in an unfamiliar part of a city that soaked daily in the blood of its citizens. How people would jeer if they knew: Rosaline the proud, who considered herself so much better than others, shivering with fear in a back alley. I felt humbled—but also angry. I hated my own helplessness.

And then I heard, oh so faintly, what sounded like a low laugh, a chuckle, and then footsteps walking slowly away until I could hear them no more.

I had little time to feel relief, for I was still completely lost. Well, I couldn't just stay shriveled up here in fear forever. I straightened and walked purposefully back the way I'd come (which fortunately was not the direction the retreating footsteps had gone). I didn't run, but I didn't dawdle any either, and I tried once more to focus—this time on my own memories. How had I gotten here? How could I get back to the friar's, since that was pretty much the only safe place I could think of?

It felt like hours before I finally found familiar ground and resumed running. Perhaps it had been hours; luckily, as it was early summer, I still had daylight to see by. As I fleetingly glimpsed the piazza, I saw no sign that there had been any kind of violent disturbance, no sign that two souls had perished here. If an architectural space could shake its head, this one seemed like that's what it was doing: *The people have come and gone, as they are wont to do, as they will keep doing, and I will watch them in their foolishness.*

At last, I burst through the friar's gate into his garden. "I found Romeo!"

"Hmm? Ah, yes, good," murmured the friar absently, fussing with his plants as usual. I couldn't help but notice there was a leaf stuck to the center of his forehead.

I shook my head, almost as if to dislodge the leaf by proxy as well as to refocus on the serious matters at hand. "Not good. He tried to kill Tybalt!"

"Tried?"

"He only scratched Tybalt before the Capulet was borne away by his men." The friar seemed puzzled, and I added, "But Tybalt is dead anyway! Someone else killed him and now people think it was Romeo!"

Rather than being horrified, the friar looked curious. "How do you know this?"

"I was there! I saw it happen!"

"Did no one else see who committed the murder?"

"It could only have been Capulets who saw, and they would not tell if they had seen. It was someone dressed in Capulet clothing, Friar—his own kinsman. But everyone believes it was Romeo—for all I know, Romeo believes it himself."

The friar nodded gravely. "That, he does."

I stared. "You have seen him?"

"Yes. He told me he tried to stop a fight between Tybalt and Mercutio, and then tried to get out of fighting Tybalt himself. In the confusion, Tybalt killed Mercutio, and to avenge his death, Romeo took on Tybalt. He believes he killed Tybalt—and so does Juliet."

"Then they cannot marry! Juliet would never marry her cousin's killer, if that's what she thinks he is."

"They are already married." I stared so hard I thought my eyes might pop out from my head. How had all this happened while I was lost? He continued quietly, "Before you returned from La Fortezza, I had already agreed to marry them secretly. I have just performed the ceremony."

I continued to stare. I could barely choke out, "Why?"

"Because I saw the violence of their passions—and because I thought once they were wed, I could let their families know and the marriage would have to be acknowledged. It might even have been a way to end the blood feud. Now, however…"

"Now it's *worse*! My uncle Capulet will not care that Romeo is his daughter's husband; if anything, it will make him wish for Romeo's death with even more fervor. My cousin will be a widow the same night she is a bride." I shuddered, remembering the horrible vision of my cousin in a pool of her own blood. "No one will believe *me* if I claim Romeo is innocent—nobody would even believe I was there, for why would I be?—and none of the Capulets will admit the truth if they know it. And no one else was witness."

The friar sighed, scratching his forehead. His fingers found the leaf, which he blankly gazed at for a moment and then put in his pocket. "Rosaline—have you taken a new name, by the way? I know most do."

"It's Luminosa now. Lumi is fine," I said impatiently.

"My apologies. Lumi, then. You have done your part. You kept Romeo from killing Tybalt. It is not your fault that someone else ended up doing so. Return to La Fortezza and tell Syra what happened; I think she will be merciful."

"But what about my cousin? What about Romeo? They are still doomed because of what I did—nothing has changed."

"I will handle it. I already have a plan to aid them in escaping Verona together. You need not concern yourself." He patted my shoulder reassuringly. "Now let me see about getting you back to La Fortezza."

I felt a flash of irritation at the friar. He sounded almost condescending, as though he considered his work was serious business and mine merely a child's game. I was worried, too: I had a strong feeling that instead of righting the wrongs, we were making things even worse.

Another friar, junior to Lawrence, drove me within a short walk of La Fortezza on his way elsewhere, and as I approached my hut I noticed someone standing in front of the door. A youth, certainly, small and slight, but I could not tell initially if it was a boy or a girl before me, dressed as they were in La Fortezza's long, shapeless cloak and hood despite the heat of late afternoon. The nuns were not required to wear the cloaks and usually went without them while working in the gardens; my own such garment was balled up and scrunched under my arm.

At first I said nothing, but neither did she—I was fairly sure this was a girl. Feeling like a fool, I asked, "Who are you?" with a little exasperation.

Her answer was as mysterious as her presence. "Hello, Cousin," was all she said, and she lowered the hood of her cloak.

I stared at her, trying to place her, but while I could imagine some dim family resemblance and felt a vague sense of familiarity, she looked like no one I had ever known or met. She was somewhere around my age, maybe a little younger, and could have been my relative—she had certain delicate, aristocratic features—but there was a hardness about her, something that vividly told of a life that had not been kind. From what I could see of her arms and torso when she pulled down the hood, she looked strong but wiry, her thinness hinting at malnutrition, her strength at grueling labor; bruising on the side of her face suggested a recent beating, and her general countenance reflected a sullen wariness I had seen in street beggars and lower-level servants, ever closed off and guarded against potential harm. Her fair hair was also thin, and had been tied tightly and pinned around her head so that she looked almost as shorn as I did.

She said nothing more, so I asked again, a trifle testier, "Who are you?"

As soon as I said that, I had a sudden thrill of recognition: I *had* seen that face before, perhaps more than once. Perhaps recently. "Were you *following* me today?" I nearly shouted. "You were! Why? Who *are* you?" Now I really was shouting, enraged. All my terror had been because a *girl* had been following me, deliberately trying to scare me?

But hadn't that girl been carrying a weapon? Hadn't I had good reason to be scared?

And then that girl smiled, the chilliest smile I'd ever beheld, and her voice was equally icy. "That's a more complicated question than you could ever imagine." Her speech was sophisticated and I was even more baffled to place her. "Most people call me 'girl.' Sometimes"—her smile became marginally less hard, reflecting wry amusement—"different times, they call me 'boy.' Someone I loved used to call me Fiamma Fredda—my hair like flame, my eyes ice cold, as he put it. Sometimes I use that name, sometimes I just say Freddi." The hard chill came back. "A long time ago, I was called Susan."

I felt a sudden wave of cold over me, like the cold fire of her name—one of them, anyway. Susan—there was something about *that* name. Where had I heard it before? Seeing my growing unease, she leaned a little closer.

"My real name, however, is Juliet Capulet."

PART II

Freddi

HOW I LEARNED of the story I'm telling you is even more complicated than the story itself. One tale at a time, then. My mother and my mother's nurse (who would very briefly be my own nurse) each gave birth to a daughter within a fortnight of each other. The nurse's daughter was chubby, jolly, and healthy; I, on the other hand, cried endlessly and batted scrawny limbs at whoever tried to pick me up. Within six moons came a wave of sickness through Verona, and both babes were afflicted, I far worse than she. Weak, poorly, I was not expected to live. I was taken away, and Susan—my nurse's child—was put in my place. Only the nurse and her husband knew about the switch, though my mother must have known—even a mother as self-absorbed as mine knows her own child—but all of them feared my father's wrath and power. My mother could have no more children after me, which suited her just fine; it meant her brutish bear of a husband would leave her alone at night and seek his pleasure discretely elsewhere.

Yet if I perished, they—Lord and Lady Capulet—would have no one.

Susan's father took me to La Fortezza's convent—the *real* convent, not the part where we are now—where they were to keep me comfortable for the remainder of my life. Perhaps the man felt more pity than his wife or my mother had, perhaps he knew there were healers in La Fortezza who might miraculously cure me. If so, he knew this would be a terrible thing for all of them, because the switch might be found out, but it would save my life—which is exactly what happened. The man died a few years later, so I will never know or ever get to thank him, not that he deserved much thanks. He still knew what he was doing. They all did.

Just like that, everything had been taken from me, and everyone went along with it, because it suited them just fine. Well, I will tell you something about being the lowest of the low: you no longer have anything to lose. They did heal me at La Fortezza, of course. I survived, but I had nothing, abandoned, discarded, no past, and a questionable future.

I grew healthy and strong there, sharing their labor, their roof, and their meals. The nuns were not affectionate, and they never coddled me one bit, but did everything they could for me to thrive. When it came to my education, the nuns raised me the way nuns raise any orphan, preparing me for a life of servility, humility, and no expectations. I knew nothing about the other side of La Fortezza for years. I learned no magic; instead, I learned the skills I would need to get by once the convent ridded itself of me. They had it in mind that as I was a quick learner, a hard worker, and "tolerable in appearance and demeanor," I might become a servant in a great house, though I was always welcome to live out the rest of my life at La Fortezza.

And here is where the paths of our lives, thus far so very different, converge. There were a few great houses who wanted their servants to look and speak in ways "befitting" of their rank, whatever that meant, and thus I was tutored in proper speech—and I practiced it in Latin. So I, too, took that same translation test you did.

I, however, didn't turn it in. Instead I asked the teacher if she knew of similar documents that described potions to bring out a person's forgotten memories, preferably ones that had been thoroughly tested and proven effective. You would have thought I'd asked if I could be given proof of the existence of the Holy Ghost. My question brought me to everyone's attention—including Syra's. Would it be appropriate to send a girl with an active mind and forthright will out for a life of menial servitude? Or was it better to send her to the *other* part of La Fortezza, even though her attitude has always seemed less grateful and more resentful?

I *was* resentful. They were withholding the truth from me, I knew, and at the moment I simply wanted to force them to remember the past, *my* past, to remember who brought me there and why. Syra perceived that my questions would not end there, so she let me see the whole story. You know, I am sure, what I mean: she showed my own long-ago memories, dim as they were, as well as those of others involved, and let me see and hear how I had gotten to La Fortezza.

That is how I learned of what I've just told you. Perhaps you can imagine a little of what I felt upon receiving this knowledge. Learning about magical herbs seemed so frivolous. I would not spend any more time hidden away here while someone else was living *my* life. I told Syra I must leave immediately.

"I will not stop you," was all she said in reply.

So I left La Fortezza the very next day and immediately sought out the Capulets—to be a servant. They none of them recognized me, of course. They barely looked at me. Why should they? I was just a serving wench, an orphan of eleven though I'd said I was older; I did not merit the attention of the distinguished members of a great house. That house—its grand staircase, great ballroom, huge stone fireplaces, precious artwork, the bright and airy rooms, so many of them!—all of it should have been mine.

There I planned my revenge.

I tried to, anyway, but just getting through each hour, each day, took much of my strength. I was an eleven-year-old girl put to work like I was a grown man. You have probably never considered for one moment of your life how much work goes into making that life so comfortable and easy. I've *done* that work. I've worked so hard that my body ached right down to my bones, and the only reward for my pain was even more work—or a beating. Yes, your fine noble families aren't above smacking about a mere girl if she doesn't set the table just so, or hasn't cleaned a room just right, or for no reason at all. This body was not made for that kind of life, but vows of vengeance kept me going.

Because I was the lowest of the staff, I rarely glimpsed the family members themselves. Not even my nurse laid eyes on me, which was fine since I did not want to be discovered. Every so often, however, I'd hear their voices—the nurse's hearty guffaws after telling a long story, my mother's cool, clipped tones issuing commands, and Susan, the girl who believed she was me, sweet and melodious like birdsong. There was also the bellow and roar of Lord Capulet, of course, sometimes jolly and sometimes enraged, plus any number of aunts and uncles and cousins—*you*, in fact, on occasion (oh yes, we've "met" before, so to speak). I hated all of them. I wanted to silence their voices, but I needed a plan.

I used to watch the men practice sword fighting in the courtyard sometimes. It fascinated me, and I wanted to learn. Of course, this was impossible, yet I did practice in secret. One day Tybalt found me, sword in hand, copying his moves. Crimson-faced, he yanked the weapon from my hand, pushed me roughly against a wall and threatened my virtue and my life. I was saved by Mercutio, visiting old Capulet that day. Only the greatest swordsman in Verona could have saved me from the second greatest, for that is what Tybalt would always be—and he knew it, much to his own ire. He slunk off like the pathetic creature he was, while Mercutio turned to me.

I fell in love with Mercutio that very moment. That probably surprises you; perhaps you think I am too young to know what love really is. No one is too young; we are born knowing it, even if by its absence, like I was. Yes, Mercutio was ribald and sardonic and moody, raging at the foolishness of the world one minute and shouting with laughter at it the next. No one was spared his jests, least of all those closest to him, and he saved his bawdiest jokes for the most inappropriate times and audiences.

He was also kinder to me than anyone else was. Plagued by demons himself, he recognized in me one of those people who are adept in hiding their suffering behind a mask—one of jocularity in his case, cold reserve in mine. But he did not love me in return the way I loved him, but rather only in the way a brother might love a younger sister. He loved no woman in *that* way, the way I yearned for, certainly not a too-young girl, and he made it clear he would not take advantage of my naivete.

He did teach me to use the sword, however, for which I am eternally grateful. We would practice in the courtyard at the prince's palace, where Mercutio, his kin, was staying—that's right, I have been to the palace, a place you and my imposter have never seen. Mercutio had me dress as a boy in some of his own clothes so observers would not think anything amiss; I was simply a young noble seeking instruction.

Those were the best hours of my life. Some days, after we practiced long and hard, our faces glistening with sweat, he would stand near me, and touch my face with his hand, and smile. It was a sad smile; perhaps he merely pitied the silly servant girl in her absurd infatuation with him. I liked to imagine we were both thinking the same thing: if only, if only we could be lovers, if only I were not so young and he could love someone like me. But regardless, those moments made my heart just about burst with happiness. And he was a superb teacher; if I'd had more time, Tybalt would no longer have been the second-best sword fighter in Verona. I, a servant girl merely thirteen years old, was better.

And yes, it was I who killed Tybalt, so quickly and in so unassuming a disguise no one noticed. No one but you, granted. They all believed it was Romeo, and I did not care that they did. Romeo would have done the deed, and I bore no love for him given that his stupidity got my love killed.

Tybalt was a brute, one who picked on weaker people. Romeo's mistake was his initial refusal to fight, and Mercutio knew it, because that would only provoke Tybalt all the more. Mercutio was well known as the best swordsman in Verona. Thus he knew he was safe in challenging Tybalt; Tybalt could not beat him and would not want to lose face in trying, so the two would have gone through the posturing and motions of fighting until someone got Tybalt out of it. Which, of course, wasn't what happened: Romeo stupidly tried to stop the fight and in the scuffle got his friend killed. For that, I hated him.

I had come to the piazza, dressed as a boy much like you were, because I knew Mercutio would be there, and I wanted to beg for another lesson. I found him, too late. I glimpsed his blood-soaked, lifeless form, and I turned, almost mechanically, coldly. I picked up a discarded jacket bearing Capulet colors and took my first great act of revenge.

I admit, too: I was jealous, because I knew Mercutio loved Romeo. He never told me outright—he kept it from everyone, including Romeo, for obvious reasons—but I knew all the same, and I think he meant for me to know to help me understand why he couldn't return my affection. I tell you this only as explanation, and if I find you have repeated any of it and besmirched his good name, you'll die at my hands even quicker than Tybalt did.

Regardless, Romeo's banishment sits well with me, though I had not intended for him to take the blame. Oh, had you not heard? He must leave Verona immediately and never return. It is a merciful punishment; he did, after all, fight, which Prince Escalus has forbidden by penalty of death. The fighting itself was none of my doing, and if Verona thinks he killed Tybalt, that is none of my concern. Romeo is hardly an innocent victim, and as for the idea that he still does not deserve so extreme a punishment—well, I know a great deal about undeserved suffering. Romeo gets no sympathy from *me*.

He does not love Juliet Capulet. He loves a girl who has gotten everything that was supposed to be mine and doesn't have the tiniest idea how undeserved her fortune is. All I have left is revenge.

The wedding of Paris to Juliet would have been perfect. I would find my way into the scene and declare the truth. Of course, no one would believe me at first, but I was counting on the nurse and my mother being so shocked that they could not hide their true emotions, and that would give them away. Lord Capulet would see this and demand answers. The truth would come out. Paris, outraged, would leave immediately in disgust, unwed. The House of Capulet would be humiliated.

And then I would leave them. I have no interest in taking my rightful position in that great house, though it certainly would further my revenge deliciously if I did. Think of it! The serving wench ascends to a title and wealth! But the Capulets disgust me; I do not want to be one of them.

So you see, Cousin, if Romeo and Juliet run away together, as I understand your friar is planning, it will ruin *my* plan. I can't let that happen.

Lumi

TO MY CREDIT, it must be said, I remained placid throughout this speech. When she stopped speaking and looked defiantly at me, I let a silent moment pass before quietly asking, "What do you want from me?"

I had not expressed disbelief, or asked her for some proof of this outrageous tale, and I thought my equanimity would disarm her, but she continued immediately. "I want you to stay out of my way. I don't care whether you get what you want or not; that's nothing to me as long as I get what I want." She tightened her lips into a cold sneer. "People like you usually get everything they want without having to work for it anyway. Don't interfere with my plans and perhaps we'll both be satisfied."

For a moment I barely knew how to respond. I bristled at the "people like you" condemnation—after all, I was close to losing the only thing I had ever wanted, a place at La Fortezza. But I had to admit that this girl's life had been infinitely more difficult than mine, whether her story about being Juliet was true or otherwise. Could I blame her for craving revenge against the people who made her daily life hell? What else did she have to look forward to? She could never prove she was Juliet Capulet. And if she really were Juliet, given the turns her life had taken, she would always be out of place, never her true self. Either way, her life would always be hard.

But I also knew that vengeance was the worst kind of satisfaction to pursue. Everyone would lose. At least that much of La Fortezza's lesson about doing good had taken root in me, and I could see many people being hurt and no one being helped, not even—well, I suppose I would call her Freddi since "Juliet" felt wrong and "Susan" genuinely was wrong. Freddi would lose, possibly as much as her life if the truth about Tybalt came out.

"I do have my own plans," I said, remaining placid in voice and expression. "They involve saving Romeo and—the girl I have known as my cousin. If your vengeance includes harming them, I will stop you."

She laughed mirthlessly, flung a side of her cloak open, and placed a hand on the scabbard of a sword. "*You* will stop me? And who did *you* train with?"

"Draw your weapon and find out."

I saw her hand move up and tighten on the sword's handle. I was ready. She tried to draw it out but her arm remained frozen, unable to move. Her smirk turned into an angry scowl.

"La Fortezza trained me!" I shouted, unable to resist a taunt of my own, even though what I'd said wasn't quite true. It sounded good, anyway.

My jeering must have broken my concentration just enough for her to regain power and draw her sword. I straightened my back, lifted my chin, and looked her in the eyes.

Slowly she inched toward me. I remained still. Suddenly she thrust toward my right shoulder, then my left. Feints both—she was toying with me. I did not move. Just then I didn't care if I couldn't control her and she stabbed me; more important was that I did not flinch, did not show fear. I stared unblinkingly into her eyes.

She thrust the sword at my face.

The tip stopped a hair's breadth from my left cheek, just under my eye, and did not move. Nor did I. Nor did Freddi at first, though her brows began to knit and she seemed to be trembling slightly with an effort to move.

"Enough."

It was Syra. Where had she come from? She seemed to have materialized next to me out of nowhere, though it occurred to me that I had been so intent on blocking Freddi and then blocking my own fear that I probably hadn't noticed anything else. Freddi, meanwhile, had been so intent on running her sword through my skull that she, too, had missed Syra's entrance.

Freddi drew back her sword and flung it to the ground in rage, but with Syra there, even she did not dare to do anything more than that. Syra motioned her toward a bench in the shade of an olive tree away from where we stood, and Freddi sat there readily enough, though her every muscle still seemed to hum with violent fury.

Syra continued in her usual quiet, toneless voice. "Nothing is gained by this. The two of you need to work as allies and not opponents."

Allies? Gone was my composure as I whipped my face around to stare. Was Freddi here because Syra asked her to be? "Allies?" I blurted. "That's not possible."

"The kind of magic we do here does not involve one

person inflicting spells on others. Our magic is about connection between people. You did not simply force Romeo to miss Tybalt; you had to be part of him and he you."

I blanched; I had never in my life wanted a connection with Romeo, which was why I was in this mess in the first place. "Yes, well, that's fine but she and I have different goals," I said, trying to imitate Syra's coolness and immediately failing. "And even if we didn't, I don't want to work with her and I daresay she feels the same about me."

"But you are both working for La Fortezza. Fiamma Fredda is also a candidate for the school, the same as you are."

"*Her? She* is being considered along with *me?*" I knew how that sounded—incredibly snobbish—but I couldn't help it. I was aghast. And no, it wasn't because Freddi had been a "mere servant," as many of my family would have put it. She'd *killed* a man. She was seeking revenge on a whole family. How could she possibly be a candidate for entry into La Fortezza's school? What if she got in and I didn't? That would be unendurable.

"We've seen in her the potential for both great strength and great mercy," Syra said mildly.

"Strength I can see. She's nearly as strong as a man—stronger, I daresay, than quite a few." I'd had a much harder time controlling her movements than I had Romeo's. "But mercy? I find that hard to believe given that her great ambition is to bring down the House of Capulet."

"All the more reason for mercy."

I hardly knew how to respond to this baffling remark. "And what about Tybalt?" I demanded instead. "She certainly showed no mercy to him."

Even as I said it, though, I felt ashamed. I had only assumed Syra knew about Tybalt's murder, but if somehow she didn't,

I shouldn't have been the one to tell her. And the truth, if I were completely honest, was that on some level I felt Tybalt got what he deserved. Tybalt Capulet was a vicious brute, one of the worst people I'd ever known; I had dreaded my visits to my cousin coinciding with his. He never smiled unless he was causing someone pain, never laughed unless he'd humiliated someone in a fight. Far from being appalled by what Freddi had done, I actually felt a certain amount of, well, satisfaction.

Syra was watching me carefully, and I was pretty sure she knew my thoughts at that moment. All she said, however, was, "We should all aspire to be merciful. It is one of the greatest challenges—and can have the greatest impact."

I struggled to repress a sigh. I knew now she was talking not just about Freddi but me. I was supposed to be merciful to her, to give her a chance to right the wrongs.

She continued, a little more stern. "La Fortezza is not just for those who are qualified to be here. It is also for those who most *need* to be here. No one needs guidance more than one who has never had any."

"Yes, fine, agreed," I said, knowing I probably didn't sound very sincere, "but guidance takes time and we have very little time to lose. Juliet—she who is known as Juliet—and Romeo are in grave danger."

"Indeed," said Syra, implacable as ever. "So let us begin immediately."

She called Freddi back. Without any preamble, she gave her order: "Fight."

Without hesitation, I focused, but I couldn't help noticing that Freddi seemed uncertain. "Fight her? Now? She's unarmed."

Syra did not repeat her command but continued to gaze

steadily at Freddi. That look was enough to make even Freddi cowed and obedient. She raised her sword and came at me.

I already knew I was enjoying the spectacle of a humbled Freddi too much to have proper focus on controlling Freddi's actions, and sure enough, with her first thrust the tip of the sword stopped an inch before the exact center of my forehead. Now Syra turned her gaze to me. "Again."

Freddi, a little stunned, drew her sword back as if it had been a cork she'd been struggling to release from a stubborn wine bottle. I realized that Syra had stopped her when I had failed. Freddi realized this too, because she regained her poise and readied herself again. There was an excited twinkle in her eyes; perhaps she recalled her days training with Mercutio. More likely, though, she realized she could try to kill me with complete impunity, as many times as she wanted.

Which is exactly what happened. Again and again, I stood perfectly still while Freddi ran her sword at me, and each time, just a split second before what would have been my bloody death, Syra stopped the death blow and said quietly, "Begin again."

Freddi practically chortled. She was enjoying this immensely, the fact that she had effectively killed me several times in the past hour. Well, I thought grimly, it wouldn't happen again.

Freddi swiveled, thrust, feinted, moved left, lunged forward, dodged right, whirled around me. It was all show; her eyes were full of mockery and her lips curved in a smirk. I sensed her readying for another death blow. I locked eyes—and minds—with her. The tip of the blade shuddered, then stilled. Freddi struggled with it but it remained immobile.

Then it fell to the ground, hitting a large stepping stone with a clang.

I remained still, not even blinking.

Freddi put her hands on her hips and raised her chin. "Go on," she spat. "Gloat. You won. You beat me."

"I'm not trying to 'beat you.' And I didn't win." I now looked over at Syra. "I failed."

"Why?" she asked quietly.

"Because I very, *very* much want to gloat."

She nodded and said nothing more. I turned back to Freddi, who was looking at me like I'd just grown a tail. But through that wary incredulity I thought I perceived something else: Freddi appeared just the tiniest bit less disgusted with me.

Maybe I hadn't failed after all.

Syra finally broke into a thin smile. "You are allowed to have feelings, Luminosa, and to recognize the difficulty of mastering such feelings. La Fortezza is not about complete abnegation of the self, despite what outsiders may believe. 'Only do good' also means to do no harm to yourself. If you feel like gloating, there's no use in pretending you don't—it may even do harm. The same," she said, turning now to Freddi, "applies to the desire for revenge."

Again I could only stare. Syra was equating my need to be proud of an accomplishment with Freddi's need to humiliate or—and?—murder her own family.

Freddi was speaking now. "I have never pretended to want anything else. You knew that when you released me. Now you want me back? I just came here for the protection you offered, that's all."

Worse and worse. Not only had Syra known everything Freddi had done—of course she had—but she also apparently condoned it. I could suddenly see why Friar Lawrence had had some misgivings about La Fortezza.

Syra's face hardened visibly. "Yes," she said to me, as if I had been the one to speak and not Freddi. "Friar Lawrence has definitely made things more difficult for you, as he is wont to do. I suggest you start with him. You"—and now she addressed Freddi—"will accompany Luminosa. You did not really come here for protection, after all."

Clearly neither of us liked this arrangement. Obviously neither of us had a choice.

⁘

"I feel like I've been to this church more times in one day than I have all year."

Stony silence from Freddi. Fine, I thought, tearing hungrily into the crusty bread and tangy cheese that Corri, again driving, had provided. I needed Freddi to accompany me, according to Syra, but beyond her presence I needed nothing else from her at the moment. She could be sullen and sneering to her dark heart's content, and I wouldn't need to instruct her to let me do the talking.

This time I found the friar in the vestry, a book in each hand and another under an arm. He nearly dropped all three when he saw me.

"Why have you returned?" His voice was gently exasperated, though more to be humorous than reprimanding. "My apologies, Luminosa, but I assure you that I have made arrangements to aid in their reunion and escape. Why do you still seek them out?"

He did not scold, nor did he seem annoyed or suspicious. Once again I felt as if he saw me as a child trying to help put out a raging fire with a small goblet of water. Cute and well-meaning, but the real work would be done by him. Well, if it would get him to listen to me, I'd play the role he'd cast me in.

"Oh, Friar," I stammered, hand on heart, eyelids fluttering with fear, "I told you I had a—I don't know what you would call it—prophecy, or vision, about their future. About what could happen if we don't stop it. But I didn't tell you the details. It was horrible! Oh, Friar, they are doomed."

He gestured toward a chair, then hastily cleared it of books before repeating the gesture. "Sit down, Lumi, and tell me slowly and calmly. What was this vision?"

His own slow, calm speech was only making me more agitated. I did not sit; I had to make him see just how urgent this was. "It was in a small room, and dark, and—I don't know how to describe it, but I felt sick being there, like the air was poisonous."

The friar's face paled, and he set his armload of books carefully on a table. "A small, dark room—like a..." He faltered.

"Like a tomb," I said. "Yes, that's it."

Now the friar looked sick. "You're sure they... that it was..."

"Yes. It was a tomb, it was Romeo and Juliet, and they were dead, he by poison and she by a dagger. Suicides!" The friar visibly cowered, as if I'd tried to hit him.

"It can't be," he whispered. "It cannot happen that way. I had everything planned just so."

"What plan? Please tell me, Friar. I must know."

"I gave her a potion for a death-like sleep. I timed it perfectly: she would take it at night, be moved to the Capulet crypt the next morning, and awaken that night. I have sent a messenger to inform Romeo, and he will meet me at the crypt tonight when she awakens. I timed it right—I know I did, Rosaline. It cannot fail."

He sounded like he was trying to convince himself as much as me. My vision had shaken him thoroughly (his slip in using my old name was annoying but telling), and I could not keep pretending to be a fearful little girl looking to him for guidance. Clearly he had none. "What if it does fail? It *will* fail, according to my vision. What if Juliet wakes up too soon? In a sealed tomb, once she begins breathing normally, she'll suffocate." I realized that wouldn't explain the dagger, but then another thought came to me. "Or what if Romeo misses your message? He might hear of Juliet's supposed death and rush to the tomb to be with her."

He shook his head fervently. "I have sent Friar John with a message telling Romeo everything he needs to know and do."

"And do messengers never get delayed or stopped?" I almost couldn't believe my impertinence; my father, normally an even-tempered man, would surely have given me a clout on the head for talking to the friar this way. My uncle Capulet would have knocked me across the room. But I was angry and desperate. "I believe the credo of La Fortezza is something like, oh, meaning to do good things is never the same as actually doing them. Wouldn't the church agree?"

The friar stared at me, and for the first time in my acquaintance with him he looked, not angry, but cold. Gone were his jovial smile, his kind eyes, his tranquil and gentle demeanor— everything that made him different from other friars and beloved by his flock as a result. He had never been one to preach fire and brimstone; he preached healing and helping others. Now his eyes looked almost icy. "You sound like her. Syra. I feared this would happen."

"Feared what would happen? Why did you let me go there if you 'feared' something would happen?"

"I had an agreement with La Fortezza, and I honored that agreement. Had I known—"

"Friar, forgive me, but I am telling you something now so that you won't need to say 'had I known' later. Romeo and Juliet are still in great danger. My co—" I had almost said "cousin" but continued smoothly, "companion and I have been instructed by Syra to get them out of danger. I acknowledge and appreciate all you have done, but now we ourselves must do our part."

I had hoped that would be a graceful way for us to get out of there. Clearly the friar would be no help, but I had no wish to antagonize him. At that moment, he looked merely puzzled.

It was only then that I realized Freddi was no longer there.

Freddi

I WAS BACK IN the House of Capulet. I knew all the ways to get in and out of this house without being seen—I'd decided on the hidden door in the wine cellar this time—and now I was free to find the nurse. This was a risk, of course, but I figured everyone would be too distracted by their bereavement to notice me, and anyway, if they recognized the former servant who had left abruptly, they gave it no consideration. Besides, I had the servant's way of knowing how to be invisible.

I found the nurse's room and slipped silently through the door. I heard her rasping breath before I saw her, hidden as she was under a mountain of tattered blankets, and I slowly approached the bed. I had to tread carefully, in all ways. I had been in the presence of the dying many times, and I suspected she too was nearing her final hour, which meant a sudden shock might bring death prematurely to her chamber. I needed her alive, at least for a little while. I stopped moving when I finally saw her, face gray and crumpled like an old handkerchief, trembling with anguish, this woman who gave me away. "I have news of Juliet," I began, whispering so that she would not know who spoke and I would not be heard outside the room.

I did not have to worry about how to continue. In her agitation, her mind had fixed itself on the very subject I wished to bring up.

"Oh, poor Juliet. Poor babe. She was such a wee thing. Hard to believe such a helpless little one nearly killed her mother and herself coming into this world. Her life never did go well from the moment of her birth." She gave a wail of sorrow, surprisingly robust given her frailty.

And then, without my prompting her at all, she sat up and burst out with all the things I had planned on forcing her to confess. "Oh what could we do? She was dying, poor girl. My lady could not bear another. If I gave her my Susan, I thought everyone would win. My lord and lady had a child. My child lived in luxury, and she was still my own dear girl, and I could be with her every day, and—"

I broke in. "Not everyone won."

"No," the woman sobbed, sinking back weakly into the bed. "Everyone still lost. We lost our Juliet anyway."

I moved even closer and pulled the hood from my head, the scarf from my face.

"Juliet is not dead."

Such a thing to behold, the struggle in that woman's face—confusion, doubt, hope, joy, one after another then all at once. I leaned closer.

"Juliet *did not die.*"

Every conflicting emotion instantly vanished, replaced with pure shock, as I fixed my eyes on hers. *She will not survive this revelation*, I thought, and quickly backed away, lowered my eyes, and continued. "The friar gave her a sleeping potion, to mimic death until she is reunited with Romeo in the crypt. They will escape together."

The old woman reached out a trembling hand, barely seeming to register my words. "You—you are—you say she—"

"She is alive. Your Susan is alive. As is Juliet Capulet." And before the color could drain any more from her face, before I fully realized what I was doing, I whispered, "And she forgives you."

The old woman—my nurse—sighed and closed her eyes.

She died, minutes later, with a smile on her lips, absolved of her sins. She, the root of all the suffering I'd endured, the only one left who could have told of the switch between Susan and me, who could have helped me right those wrongs.

But I'd always known nothing would ever come easy to me, and I'd never put any faith in relying on others for help. I would have to do this myself, once more. And somehow I felt an odd satisfaction in that. I did not feel cheated in my vengeance because of what happened between me and the nurse. I merely felt the need to move on.

As I was making my way from her chamber and back down to the wine cellar (probably the last time I would be in this house, I reflected with indifference), I caught a glimpse of Lady Capulet on the grand staircase. She descended like a long-time inhabitant of hell might trudge mindlessly to its depths. She, who had always prided herself on her youthful beauty, now looked haggard, her eyes dull. She moved the way I've seen men in fights move when they've all but given up trying to protect themselves because they know it's no use—a weary, defeated stagger.

She was not yet 30 years old.

Was she this sorrowful when she thought I had died? Or did she see Susan, hear her being called by my own name, and instantly forget all about me?

But as I watched her, the same feeling came over me, albeit less intensely, as I'd experienced with the nurse. I felt pity. My mother unquestionably had suffered, and suffered the worst loss a mother could. Whether she experienced it once or twice hardly mattered at this point.

At that moment she happened to look up, saw me watching her, and locked her eyes on mine. I could easily have rushed away, but for just a few seconds, I stayed like that.

She looked away and continued to descend the stairs.

She was weak, I reflected, making my way down the servants' stairs. My mother was to be pitied far more than hated. She feared my father's wrath so much she entered into a lifelong lie. Perhaps I had inherited my father's capacity for anger, I mused, but somewhere in me I knew there was something else besides rage.

Lumi

---✦---

PARIS WAS NOT supposed to be here. Why in the world was he? He owed my cousin—or, rather, the girl he thought was Juliet—nothing, nor was anything from the house of Capulet any longer due to him. He should have been well on his way to find some other rich young girl to make his bride. Instead he was here, at the family crypt, to lay flowers on his dead not-bride's tomb. He had even declared aloud, in a voice choked with tears, that he would return each evening with flowers for her, in her honor. And because of this sweet, kind, loving gesture, he might very well be another corpse within that tomb if I couldn't figure out how to handle this.

I had left the friar stubbornly insisting that his plan would work and that he would wait at the church for Romeo to arrive, according to his letter, before bringing the young groom to Juliet. My own plan had been to get to the tomb first, to calm and assist Juliet if she awoke early, or, if otherwise, to get Romeo to stop for just a moment before the fool went and drank the poison

I'd foreseen. It would be just long enough for my cousin to awaken from her death sleep, just long enough for them to be reunited, to leave the crypt joyously and escape with Friar Lawrence's help. With Paris there in the way, understanding neither Romeo's innocence nor his marriage to Juliet, there would certainly be a fight.

If Romeo killed Paris—and that seemed a likely outcome—a truly innocent man would be dead. Tybalt had deserved his fate. Everyone knew he'd end up dead in a fight someday. But Paris? He was not a fighter. Moreover, if my cousin saw his slain body there, she might feel a needle of doubt amidst her great rapture at being rescued by her beloved. Here would be one man, a good one who died for her sake, and another who killed that good man (along with, as far as she knew, her own kin, Tybalt). Had she chosen right? Perhaps that question might haunt her for the rest of her life, and then their lives would still be ruined, and once again I would have failed to avert the disaster.

"What is *he* doing here?"

The voice seemed to bellow in my ear and I all but fell over, though it had been just a whisper. It was Freddi. What was *she* doing here?

She grinned. "For that matter, what am I doing here? And what was I doing before? I had some business to finish at the Capulets'."

She did not seem inclined to give details. "Anyone dead?" I said flippantly, though as soon as I said it I wished I hadn't since the answer might very well have been "yes."

"Yes," she whispered back coolly, "but not by my hands. I'm here to help. Looks like you'll need it."

I left it at that, because I had more pressing matters to worry about. We both watched Paris for a moment in silence. I turned to Freddi and was about to speak when I noticed something odd about her face. The hardness had softened, her eyes had widened, and she gazed at the young man with a look that reminded me strongly—bizarrely—of Juliet. She sensed me staring and both of us changed our expressions back to serious and cool.

"You handle Paris," she hissed. "Get him away from the crypt. I'll take care of Romeo. No, I don't mean like that," she said testily at my look. "I'll *stall* him." She looked curiously at me. "Do you know what you're doing?"

Always with her, skepticism tinged with contempt. And to think I had been called disdainful. Still, I couldn't blame her for staring. Instead of magic, I had decided to fall back on plain old trickery. As we spoke, I was draping my arms and hair with delicate mosses and ferns in hopes of creating an otherworldly apparition, or at least to sufficiently disguise my worldly, boyish one. Up close I looked ridiculous, but far enough away, seen with lovelorn eyes, speaking in a pretty good imitation of Juliet's voice (she and I used to play tricks on the servants by pretending to be each other)—well, I hoped this would be enough to do what needed to be done.

All I said was, "I am 'handling Paris'," adding in my mind, *And I'm figuring out just how to handle you.*

I moved slowly and silently away, looking for a good place to set my candle. A large rock with a small flat section looked just about perfect, so I put the light there, took a deep breath, and turned back toward Paris.

At first he didn't see or hear me, so intent was he on his lovelorn ministrations. I rustled my flora finery and began to whisper: "Count Paris. My dearest, would-have-been husband. Look upon me."

He whirled around, his face both anguished and appalled.

"Who art thou who intrudes upon this sacred ground? Name yourself, villain!"

"It is I, Juliet."

He froze. With the candle behind me, he could not see my features, and my silhouette had become a strange and (I hoped) ghostly form. I spoke softly now instead of whispering, still keeping my voice carefully disguised. "Count Paris, it is I, Juliet. Do not be frightened. My soul awaits ascension to the heavenly realm, but I linger here only to give you one last message."

"Juliet! Juliet, my love! Command me and I shall do your bidding."

Perfect—he'd better mean it, I thought grimly. "Count Paris, I beg you, do not waste your life away mourning for me. I am honored by your love and devotion; now do me the even greater honor of turning your love to the living. Return to your home and do not come back to this place of death."

He bowed deeply, hands clasped to his heart. His chivalry surprised me, I admit, and I realized that Juliet and I had perhaps been very wrong about the count. But still, the strangeness and excessiveness of his gallantry and fervor irked me, much the way Romeo's had. What, after all, had Juliet really been to Paris? His wife-to-be, yes, but he barely knew her. It had been more or less a business transaction, this marriage, and he'd spent no more than a few hours in her presence. How could a few hours' acquaintance lead one to grand gestures such as this, vowing to place flowers on her grave forever? The absurdity of it annoyed me. Wealthy young men! Freedom was wasted on them. He could do anything, and instead—this nonsense.

Fortunately, it seemed *this nonsense* was over, as I had been successful in mimicking my cousin and getting the count to be on his way. I wished him well as I watched him go.

Freddi

BEAUTIFUL, LOVELORN PARIS, who might have been my husband. I watched him follow the supposed apparition of Juliet and thought Susan was a fool. She could have had everything, but apparently that wasn't good enough for her. I watched the count go toward the voice he thought was Juliet's (how many others were going to pretend they were me, anyway?) and I sighed once more with silent resentment.

It was lucky Lumi acted when she did, for no sooner had Paris disappeared into the dark when I heard steps approaching that had to be Romeo's. I darted out and stood before the door to the crypt, weapon drawn. The moment he laid eyes on me, I took a fighting stance. "Stop."

"Stand aside! I have no quarrel with you and do not wish to kill you but I will if you stand between me and my love."

I wanted to laugh. Even with the fire of passion running through his body, Romeo was no match for me. It would have been too easy to take him down, but my job here was to stall him until the friar appeared. I sighed and took a step toward Romeo.

He was a decent fighter—Paris would have stood no chance at all—but he wasted way too much energy in unnecessary motion, whirling and flailing when he should have kept coiled up to spring. Tybalt, I recalled, had the same defect—many men did, which was why women made better fighters, Mercutio had observed. *This is why they are not allowed swords. No man would admit that his woman is better at handling his weapon than he is, for she might choose to handle other men's weapons as well* was how he put it with a guffaw. Mercutio, I reckoned, would have been proud of me right now, even if I was fighting his forbidden beloved. When I figured enough time had passed (honestly, I was getting bored), I knocked his sword from his hand and pushed him into kneeling with a swift kick in the chest.

Romeo bowed his head. "I beseech you for this one last mercy: lay me in that tomb with my love, Juliet."

Again I half wanted to burst out laughing, half wanted to kill him right then and there for saying such a stupid thing. "You idiot," I spat instead. "Your 'Juliet' lives." I uttered the name with a sarcasm he would, of course, never comprehend. "The friar gave her a sleeping potion. She will awaken shortly. Do you want her to rise up from her death-like sleep only to see your bloodied, mangled corpse? You will truly kill her in that case."

He began to tremble, his eyes wide. "Juliet—alive?"

I could have run my sword through him with ease at that moment, so much had he dropped his guard ("Yes, she lives—right here, as you die!"), but it wasn't worth having to clean my blade for the little satisfaction I'd get from such an easy victory.

"Go quickly, Montague. Be with your bride when she returns to life, and then be off with you both." *Lest I change my mind this instant*, I thought with bitterness, watching him scramble for the entrance to the crypt.

Of course he would get what he wanted. He had wanted to marry Juliet, so he married her, or at least the girl everyone believed was her. Would he have wanted to marry Susan, daughter of a lowly servant? It hardly mattered, since he got what he wanted regardless. He had wanted to kill Tybalt, so Tybalt died. He should have been killed himself, but received a truly merciful banishment instead. He did everything he could to ruin his chances of being reunited with his bride, yet still people went out of their way to help them to be together. He had no idea of his fortune; he would go the rest of his life having no idea, simply reaping the rewards of his position in the world.

But most of all, he would not become embittered at far too young an age, as I had been.

Lumi

—✳—

"YOU HAVE DONE well," Syra said once, yet again,
I was back at La Fortezza, back in my little room,
though it had only been mine for a short time. "The
vision did not materialize; Romeo and Juliet did not perish in
the tomb. They are alive and together and free. You also showed
wisdom and compassion in dealing with Paris. Commendable,
Luminosa."

"Yet Romeo is still believed to have murdered Tybalt. I
cannot imagine my uncle and his Capulets will be satisfied with
his merely being banished, especially when they learn about the
marriage and escape. They will say Romeo ravished my cousin,
forced her to marry him. Even if Friar Lawrence reveals his
part, their blood lust will smother all reason." Something else
occurred to me just then. "And Paris! Paris will find out that
Juliet did not die. He will almost certainly seek her out again,
and Romeo, lest he look like a great fool. There are still so
many loose ends, Syra."

"None of that is your responsibility."

I stared at her. "Their lives will still be hard. I pushed Friar Lawrence to tell me where they were going once he'd helped them escape—he said they were aiming for Mantua, trying to get work as servants. Servants! Even if the Capulets don't find them right away, both of them have lived in luxury all their years—how will they make it? Ask Freddi, she'll be happy to tell you what a hard life that is."

"No longer your responsibility," she repeated.

I was silent for a moment. Syra was too, and she could clearly wait a lot longer than I could in that silence. "And what about Freddi?" I wasn't even sure where Freddi was at that moment; I had been escorted to my hut to meet with Syra as soon as we entered the gate and had no idea where my cousin had been taken.

"Also no longer your responsibility."

I looked carefully at Syra. Was this another test? But she smiled faintly and turned to leave.

And yet, watching her form become a shadow in the bright sunshine of the courtyard, I knew it wasn't over yet.

PART III

Susan

IT HAPPENED. I found my true love, and we were together at last.

Our families still desired to annihilate each other. Disease still ravaged the land. That he and I met and loved and escaped together meant little to anyone else—but it meant everything to us.

Sometimes when I looked at my husband, I realized how little I truly knew him, and that only increased my love. I recalled a certain conversation I had with my cousin Rosaline, only a few hours before I met my Romeo, in fact, in which she said I wouldn't know the person I fell in love with and that would be part of the reason I fell. I didn't know what she meant at the time—I am not even sure she knew the whole of her own wisdom—but I understood now. I didn't know Romeo but my love for him meant that whatever I discovered would be received by me with compassion and gracious acceptance, and the same would be true for what he discovered about me. Is that not truly one of the greatest things about love? Isn't that what we all truly want? Does it really matter how it happens, so long as it *can* happen?

But practical things matter too, and we had a lot of these to address. We could no longer go to Mantua as planned, since that was the first place they would look for us. We instead headed for Padua. Balthazar, Romeo's loyal servant, had heard of a country house just outside the town that needed additional help for a large party its lady would be hosting within the month. He supposed we might be well hidden there, though we would have to convince the lady of the house—"A Signora Nera, wife of a prosperous gentleman, both very well thought of in Padua"—that we were lifelong servants.

"Romeo, you are strong and quick, you should be able to handle the work. And Juliet—"

"I would not have my lady do hard labor!" Romeo exclaimed. This was more than gallantry; I saw real worry on his face, concern that he had taken me away from a life of comfort into one of servitude and suffering, and that I might soon regret agreeing to it. "Perhaps we could say she is ill?"

"Then they will not have her, or you. This area has recently been stricken with the Black Death, as you well know. The citizens are wary of its return."

"I will be fine, my love," I broke in, adding, "And *we* will be fine—I will not give away our ruse." I had a feeling this was going through both men's minds though they would never say it to me. They thought it would be impossible for the delicate daughter of Lord Capulet to pass for a coarse serving girl. I had a few surprises for them.

With no brothers or sisters, I had no one to play with as a child, so I had spent much of my time with my nurse's husband, chasing farm animals around the grounds, and with her older children (she had a great many), who also served my father's house. My mother frowned on these activities, of course, but she invested very little of her time in scolding me (if I'm honest, in raising me at all—she left that to Nurse), so I was able to pick up a lot of their speech and mannerisms. Still, though, I knew an observant person would easily be able to pick out the aspects of my mien, posture, movements, and speech that marked me as nobility.

I am sure Nera was suspicious the moment she encountered me, though the only sign of this was a slight, curious upturn of the corners of her lips. ("She's nobody's fool," Balthazar had warned us.) If she suspected, she did not particularly object. Perhaps she liked the idea of a certain regalness in her servants; some families did, after all. ("Fools!" I could hear my father bellow. "Servants must know their place." And my mother would nod primly in rare agreement.)

In any case, we had found ourselves at a beautiful house in the country—a newer house, which again I knew my parents would have sniffed and scoffed at, but as warm and inviting as its lady was. Indeed, beautiful Signora Nera met with us herself, an unusual thing for a lady to do (still more to sniff and scoff about!), with a radiant smile and welcome.

"I do not know how much has been explained to you about why your services are needed," she said. "You have been told I am hosting a grand party, but there are some particulars you need to understand. My younger sister and I both married within a short time of each other. Both of us wed good, prosperous men, and since then she and I have engaged in something of a merry battle. We pick an agreed-upon theme, and then each of us in turn hosts a lavish party based on that theme.

Whoever throws the grandest party wins. The score stands at one and one. I won 'Greeks versus Romans' while she won 'childhood'—she has always been childish so that one was no surprise. Plus she cheated."

My eyes widened in surprise and she laughed charmingly. "Oh I cheated too. We both sent spies to see what the other was planning. Well, this time spying doesn't matter: she has thrown the 'White Party' and I will be throwing the 'Black Party.' Her name, after all, is Bianca, and I call myself Nera, so the theme works perfectly. Everything at my party will be deliciously dark, beautifully black, and I want everything as gorgeous as the night." She looked approvingly at Romeo and me. "You two will do just fine for serving guests."

"Thank you, my lady," we both stammered, very nearly in unison, and she laughed with delight.

"Curtis will show you to the servants' quarters. My husband, Signor Petruchio, is traveling at present but will return on the morrow. Curtis, see to them."

At the name Petruchio, I felt a sudden fear grip me, such that I followed Romeo and Curtis almost blindly, barely noticing my surroundings or what was being said. The moment we were alone, I hissed to Romeo, "This may be a bad place for us to stay. There is a Signor Petruchio from Verona who is a friend of my father. He was at the party the night we met, and I think he has a country house near Padua! If it is the same man, he may recognize me." Then I reflected for a moment. "No, it cannot be. My father's friend is married to a woman named Katherina, not Nera."

"His is not an uncommon name," Romeo said, adding with a tender smile, "Do not worry, dearest. Our stars have been lucky ones so far."

It was, in fact, the same Petruchio. I recognized him when he showed up unexpectedly early that same night, not two hours after our own arrival. Whether he recognized me was hard to say—he hardly even noticed me, or Romeo, or anyone or anything else. His eyes were on his wife, his words solely for her, his entire presence—and it was a vibrant, hearty one—revolved entirely around her.

"Dearest Nera, I have bought you the prettiest gown from Venice, the only gown good enough for your beauty, for none other was worthy of the honor."

"A new gown, Husband! We are spending as extravagantly as if we had ten times your wealth! Would you have me wear a beautiful gown while eating crust crumbs for a year?"

"Very well, Wife, I shall tear it to shreds so that we may burn it in the fire for fuel!" he bellowed.

Her tone turned beseeching. "Oh Husband, your generosity overwhelms me. Do not destroy the gown; I shall wear it with a humble smile upon my unworthy face."

"Your face is worth all the treasures of heaven, my love," he cooed.

"Hmm," she suddenly sniffed. "Would that we had all heaven's treasures if you are to go roaming Italy like you do."

I knew servants were supposed to be invisible, but I couldn't help gaping at them openly. Were they insane? Why were they going on in this strange manner? When Petruchio finally left the room, dragging Romeo along and blowing his wife a half dozen kisses as he went, Nera glanced at me and I could not hide my astonished stare in time.

"You no doubt think us quite mad."

"Not for me to say, madam."

"Come now," she said, picking through the piles of gifts

her husband had brought. "I was given to understand that you are newly married. Surely you must know what we are about. Or perhaps you are too new to this. You are quite young—I imagine he is your first and only love? Well, Petruchio is mine as well, but I have learned a great deal since he first courted me."

"You see, this is what we do: we *play*. He pretends he's lord and master of the house, all bluster and swagger and bravado, while I pretend I'm his sweet, docile, doting wife." She picked up an elegant pair of black leather shoes and blinked rapidly with wide eyes and tilted head, a parody of a doting wife. "Sometimes we switch that, though: I throw things and scream and act like a shrew, he acts like I'm the most amazing treasure he has ever beheld and he'll do anything to please me." She leaned forward as if we were in a public place and might be overheard, whispering, "And sometimes *I'm* the lord and master. And he is whatever I want him to be. The first time we played at that was when I gave myself the name Nera, and I liked it so much that I use it always now." She leaned back again, eyes twinkling. "We're *playing*. And it's the most fun I've ever had in my life."

She tossed the shoes aside and poured some wine from a decanter, offering me the glass. Scandalized, I shook my head— had she forgotten I was supposed to be her servant? (Had she known I wasn't really one all along?) She shrugged and drank the wine herself. "I don't often give advice but when I do, I make it count," she added and smiled as if some amusing memory had come back to her. "So I will tell you this, and I hope you heed it well: think of love as a series of parts you play together. And if it should get to the point where it no longer feels playful as it is, take on different roles. But remember that these are, in fact, roles. When he must depart, say death would be preferable to his leaving of you, and he will say the same—and then when he leaves (because of course he will leave anyway), don't throw yourself down a well; put on a pretty dress and throw a party."

I was so fascinated with what she was saying that I myself forgot my servant's role and addressed her like an equal. "But you're saying this is all false, what we do when we're in love. It isn't false—our feelings are real!"

"Oh no, no, my dear, I am not saying that at all. Of course your feelings are real. What you *do* about it, however—that's where playing comes in. It isn't false—just the opposite, in fact. You control your play. No one can make you do it or anything else."

I laughed, then covered my mouth with my hand, realizing this might have seemed rude. Nera smiled encouragingly. "What makes you so merry, child?"

"You sounded a little like my cousin just now. 'Why must a girl only be a wife? Why should that be her one and only option?' She was always going on and on about things like that—having control, having choices. She—" I froze. I had unthinkingly mimicked Rosaline's lofty tone and slipped entirely out of my serving girl's accents and back into my own.

Nera did not look surprised in the least. "We are always playing," she said gently, "for one reason or another. We might as well enjoy it."

Had she known all along? If so, she clearly did not care.

She poured a little more wine for herself and gestured at the decanter with a *you sure you don't want some?* look. "My sister and I are playing, too, when it comes to that, with our parties. We did not get along when we were growing up, but once we both married and left our father's house, we entered into a friendly competition. Bianca has always been competitive. She had so many suitors, men lining up for a glimpse of her fair face, but she pretended she cared for none of them. And she didn't; she cared more about the fact that every man who came to our door came there for her and not me. She would pretend to be magnanimous by telling me she would 'let me have' any of them I wanted, but what girl wants to hear *that*? Getting her younger sister's castoffs because they weren't good enough for her? She was not being generous; she was only acting. It was cruelty, not kindness."

"When a man finally came for me and me alone, and when that man turned out to be the best husband I could ever want—and when her own marriage, sadly, did not quite live up to her expectations—well, she needed something to win at again, or at least try to win at."

Having no siblings myself, I had a hard time understanding how one sister could behave this way to another. As if reading my thoughts, Nera continued, "Oh you have not heard the worst of it. I was truly beastly toward Bianca when we were growing up, far worse than she ever was to me. I *was* jealous of her beauty and popularity, frustrated that no suitors ever came for me, and angry that she was perfectly aware of all this. And the longer it went on, the more she played the part of the good, sweet daughter whom every man wanted, in contrast to the bad-tempered wench no man would come near. And the worse I got. I was truly 'nera' to her 'bianca.'"

"Signora Nera, forgive me, but I find it difficult to believe anyone would think you bad tempered when you are so merry," I couldn't help but exclaim.

She chuckled. "Oh I was. Ask anyone in Padua; they wouldn't be wrong. I'd throw a chair at you as soon as look at you if I was in a bad mood—and my mood was always bad. What changed all that was my husband, his love for me and mine for him. And now it is my sister whose life is pitiable, not mine. But nobody wants to be the object of pity, so instead I offered her new roles for us to play. We are equals in competition. At least"—and here she winked, draining her glass—"until I thoroughly break her by winning with my Black Party."

∽

That night, and many nights afterward, I mulled over what Nera had said about her marriage—her *playing*, as she put it. *When he leaves, don't throw yourself down a well... throw a party.* It sounded like madness to me. When Romeo had to leave me the morning after our wedding night to prepare for our escape, I had not wanted to live another minute. Of course, that was a different situation entirely—he wasn't leaving on business but because he'd be killed if he stayed. And yet, the idea of playing kept coming back to me.

Romeo's courtship of me had seemed nothing like playing at all. It had been intense, wonderful but serious, life-and-death serious. Our lives together were still just that serious, in fact— Romeo had slain Tybalt and my family would never forget that for as long as there were any Capulets left to remember. Would we ever get to the point where we could *play*? Where we could delight in each other's company without feeling like everything we did was fraught with peril? What would it be like to savor a quiet evening together instead of feeling like we had to gorge ourselves on the moments we had together because there might not be any more such moments tomorrow?

I moved closer to my husband in our bed, resting my head on his shoulder as he put his arms around me and stroked my hair. "My love," I whispered; "Yes, my love," he whispered back. Our eyes met.

He ripped away the bedclothes while I flung myself on top of him. Gorging ourselves was not such a terrible thing, after all.

✍

The night of the party arrived, and the entire house felt cloaked in mystery. I'd initially believed Nera had the more difficult challenge; the White Party seemed to me, from all the descriptions I'd heard of it from the other servants, sumptuous and opulent, a feast for all the senses. At Signora Bianca's banquet, men and women floated through rooms like clouds, and the light, bright music was like birdsong at dawn. It sounded almost heavenly. But witnessing the Black Party firsthand, I forgot everything I'd heard.

The air smelled of wood smoke. Winding strands of music entwined with murmured conversations in dark corners. Hundreds of candles in every room cast fantastical shadows from guests in black velvet and satin, and as they moved, their shadows melded together and melted away into the night. The cook's spies, as she called them, had informed her of the White Party's menu, which included delicate filets of fish with luscious cream sauces and sparkling white wines. Cook was not the least bit intimidated, for here there were roasts crusted in fragrant charred herbs, goblets of wine so deep red they appeared almost black, bowls overflowing with the sensuous curves of plums and grapes—all dark and deliciously enticing. The wine, the music, the shadows, everything flowed deliriously into the night, sweeping me along with it.

Every lavish party my parents had ever thrown faded into

insignificance in my mind. At that moment, I never wanted to be anywhere else. Nera's party was exciting and beautiful, our lives were as well, and I was here with my Romeo, who looked handsome in the black clothes Curtis had given him, a match for the lovely black dress I wore. I had never felt so happy in my life.

Lumi

---※---

I HAD NEVER FELT so certain in my life that I was head-
ing toward complete disaster. The two of us, Freddi and I,
two *girls*, were about to take on everyone from the House of
Capulet and possibly a few from the House of Montague wanting
in on the action. If the two of us had figured out where Romeo
and Juliet had gone, others almost certainly would as well.

The only positive was that for the first time, I was glad it
was, in fact, the two of us. I still didn't trust Freddi, but now
I could see her fighting skills as an asset. I still believed she
harbored an agenda to wipe out all the Capulets she could, but
if that helped me protect the girl I knew as my cousin and her
new husband, all the better. If it helped protect *me*, better
still. I had no desire for an ironic destiny of dying just when
I'd gotten what I wanted.

I had asked Syra for the use of a coach. I fully expected
her to turn me down, since she had to know why I wanted
it. Again, she surprised me, nodding an instant agreement and saying nothing more. That

was the easy part; the hard part was figuring out what in the world I would do when I found them. Much to my own shock, the first thing I wanted to do was ask Freddi to join me. Here *she* surprised me by agreeing just as quickly as Syra had, though I suppose I should have figured on her acceptance: we were going where the Capulets would be going too, and what better opportunity for total vengeance could she hope to find? They would find Juliet married to the enemy, they would demand blood, they would discover that the young Capulet girl they thought they were defending had actually been a fraud all along. Certainly the prospect of all that happening outweighed the strong dislike Freddi had of my company.

And so toward Padua we went, my cousin and I, driven this time not by Corri but some other gray-cloaked figure I did not recognize. This was disappointing; I would have loved for Corri to let the horses have a good, fast run, since we desperately needed to get to Romeo and Juliet before the Capulets did. I had been counting on a silent journey so that I could try to figure out a plan, but once again Freddi surprised me by saying, within minutes of our departure, "She should have married Paris. I would have."

I was taken aback at this unexpected opener, but I smiled and said lightly, "It seems we have one thing in common: lack of regard for Romeo as a husband. The list ends there, though. I would not have Paris either."

"Then you're as big a fool as she is." She peered at me curiously. "You would not have any, I believe. Too superior for love, isn't that right?"

"Too indifferent, but you can believe what you want. I know you will anyway."

Now she leaned forward and made her voice a husky tease.

"What about desire? What about a man in your bed to keep you warm at night, whether he is your husband or another's or no one's at all?"

I knew she was trying to shock me, thinking I must have been prudish and naive given my upbringing. She no doubt knew all kinds of vulgar, ribald stories given *her* upbringing, or at least her experiences after she left the convent, and if I showed any reaction she would gleefully tell them to make me squirm and blush. "A bed is a confinement, more so when a man is in it with you, taking up what little space and comfort there is. I will not be confined; I desire more than that."

She laughed throatily, sounding more like a washerwoman than a daughter of the House of Capulet. "She desires more, the lusty wench! What would you have, two men? One for day and one for night? Or would it be one for ordinary days and one for special occasions?"

"None ever. I have chosen another path for myself. And," I added, "I am fortunate enough that I have gotten to choose. There may be many more like myself who have not."

That silenced her for a moment, as I thought it would. She liked reminding people like me that we had not done anything to deserve the good things in our lives, for obvious reasons. She had done nothing to deserve her abandonment as a baby; she had been as innocent as a person who suffers can be. She knew I understood this now, and I felt her bitter resentment toward the world, or at least toward me, easing a little.

When she spoke again, her voice was different, more thoughtful. "For all their wealth, their name, their power, it seems my mother and father never had it. For all their ignorance and vulgarity, my nurse and her husband apparently did. Love. In my short time at that great house, I've seen both men and women brought to ruin by it, yet others for whom it was the best thing in their lives, the thing that kept them going. That is a thing worth pursuing, and I have just as good a chance of getting it as anyone else.

"For years, the only thing I hoped for was revenge. But that kind of hope is poison to the soul. When I met Mercutio, there was something else for me to live for. I wanted to be loved. That I wasn't, by him, and have not been yet by anyone else, was painful but not poisonous, because it showed me something I didn't know was possible: I could love someone, and not just hate everyone forever. And if that was possible, maybe someone might love me back."

I was fairly stunned at this revelation, and it suddenly struck me that this Juliet and the one who took her place, though they were not related and had never actually met face to face, nevertheless had this one thing very much in common: they both valued love more highly than anything else.

Hoping I would not offend, I said, "You and Susan would have been good friends, I think. You would have been more like cousins—or even sisters—than she and I were."

I feared this might bring back Freddi's defensive coldness, but she merely looked away out the dark window and said, "Well, then, I suppose it's a good thing we are meeting at last."

At last (at *long* last, it seemed—why could we not have gotten Corri instead of this pokey driver who barely seemed awake?), we reached the outskirts of Padua and the house lay ahead of us. I was not even sure this was the right place to be looking, as the last information we'd received from the friar was only that the couple were planning to go there, not that they definitely would be there.

From the carriage outside the gate, the house looked bizarre. It seemed to glow, but a dark glow, if that makes any sense. I could hear music and voices, though everything was hushed, the way things sound in thick mist. What were we getting into? I thought wryly of all the vague, whispered gossip about La Fortezza, that "strange convent" that might not have been quite as *holy* as it ought to be, that sometimes seemed more like a coven of witches than a convent of nuns. If anything appeared witchy and unholy, it was this place, the home of a wealthy gentleman during a lavish party. If you were wealthy, I supposed you could get away with it, a thought that sounded so much like something Freddi would say I almost laughed out loud.

Unfazed as ever, Freddi jumped from the carriage and adjusted her weaponry. "Looks like we beat my kinsmen," she grunted.

"Yes, and no doubt you intend to beat them even further once they arrive," I said dryly as we made our way through the gate toward the house. "As I said before, I don't care what you do as long as Romeo and Juliet are safe. To ensure that, I am somehow going to need to get 'your kinsmen' to realize that Romeo didn't kill Tybalt, that he didn't abscond with Juliet's corpse, and that Juliet married Romeo willingly, in the church under the eyes of God. To do that, we need to hold off any bloodshed until I can find them and get everyone to listen."

Freddi barked a laugh. "My job's easier. I just have to take on all those lazy wastrels who used to make my life as a servant hell."

"And hold off bloodshed." I gave her a hard look. "Freddi."

She shrugged noncommittally. I let it go. I had more immediate concerns, like how we were going to slip into a private party unnoticed—or at least without being thrown out immediately.

Before we'd even made it to the entrance, the Capulets descended. Young men on horseback, old men in carriages, dozens of them waving weapons and shouting oaths. "Here we go," Freddi muttered. She stood in front of me and drew a weapon. "Halt and lay down your swords!"

Four young Capulets stormed toward her, ignoring her command. Only one of them reached her and clashed his sword with hers. The others remained frozen, looks of confusion on their faces as they tried in vain to move.

I was gritting my teeth as I worked on them, but so far it hadn't been much more difficult to control three people than it was a single person, mostly because they were all thinking about and doing the same thing. "Your turn," I muttered to Freddi.

"Delighted," she said and thrust at the lone moving Capulet.

It looked so ridiculous, the men standing motionless in a semicircle around Freddi, waiting their turn to fight her as if following some bizarrely polite rule of warfare. This kind of spell was clearly one of the things I was most adept at, and at that point I laughed out loud, in delight at my success and because the men looked so silly.

"Lumi!" Freddi barked, and, as if for emphasis, rammed the flat side of her sword down hard on her opponent's head. He staggered backward and collapsed against a wall. She glared at me. "Pay attention!"

"Sorry, Cousin," I said. The "cousin" part just slipped out, earnestly and not sarcastically; it felt natural to me somehow. "Which do you want next?"

Freddi scanned the three frozen figures and jerked her chin at the middle one. "Him. He looks to be the boldest. The other two look ready to piss themselves and run back to their mothers."

I suppressed another chortle. What would the Capulets think if they knew this coarse, tough-talking fighter was none other than their dear, sweet Juliet? For that matter, what would they think if they knew the girl they thought was Juliet—and thought dead—was alive and married to one of their enemy?

The door behind me opened and I did not stop to see who was letting us in; I called for Freddi and we both backed our way forcefully into the house. More Capulets followed, though still only one at a time could spar with Freddi, the rest being mine. I took a quick glance around and almost lost my focus. What bizarre world had Juliet gotten herself into? All around me were figures in black clothes and black masks, drinking black drinks and watching us intently. No one moved toward us to help or away to flee, and if anything, they seemed to be enjoying the spectacle.

Well, I thought as I turned back to renew my focus on the Capulets pouring through the open doorway, at least they aren't getting in the way. I was already feeling my mental grip slipping, my hold on the Capulet fighters weakening. As good as Freddi was, she couldn't hold them all off, and nor could I. They just kept coming, lusty cries of "Romeo! Show yourself, you coward!" drowning out the music and party noises.

"Juliet!" I countered their shouts. "Juliet, it is Lu—er, Rosaline! You are in danger and we are here to help!"

Through the darkness another black-clad figure emerged,

this one small and lithe: Juliet herself. At her heels came Romeo, also in black. "Stand behind me!" yelled Freddi to them, as two more Capulets received the flat end of her sword on their heads and fell into dazed heaps at her feet.

"Lord Capulet!" I now shouted. "Your Juliet is alive!" I traded quick glances with Freddi—we neither of us could help noting the irony. "She is here and alive and well. Come and see!"

As bewildered as Juliet must have been, she grasped quickly what needed to happen. "Father! I am safe! Please tell them to stop fighting!"

A still-livid Lord Capulet shoved his way forward, eyed me with momentary surprise, then turned to Romeo. "Villain! Juliet, get away from that fiend."

"No fiend!" I yelled back. "Her husband, my lord!"

"No husband. He murdered Tybalt, ravished your cousin, forced her into this marriage, and now—" He took in the sight of his daughter carrying a large tray laden with fruit and dressed in servant's garb, and gesticulated wildly at her. "Now he forces her to live a life of shame and poverty! Stand aside or, though you be a nun, you may be harmed in our pursuit of justice!"

There was so much wrong with what he said—everything, in truth—that I didn't know where to begin. Out of the corner of my eye, I noticed a few guests exchanging amused looks at the notion that "shame and poverty" had been forced on these beautifully dressed servants, and I suspected the whole thing amused Freddi to no end. I could also sense Juliet's fury gathering steam as she readied herself to refute that she had been forced into anything against her will—a refutation that would gain nothing, since Lord Capulet would dismiss her as simply bending to her husband's will as was "proper."

Instead of addressing my uncle, I addressed the men behind him. "It was *not* Romeo who killed Tybalt. It was a Capulet. And there are those among you who *know* it was."

This was the biggest risk I'd ever taken. The men were already so inflamed with the desire to kill that this might have turned the whole place into an inferno from which none would escape. Lord Capulet's face, already crimson with rage, looked about to turn molten. But among the others there was hesitation, shuffling, and uneasiness. They knew, I thought. They knew the House of Capulet faced as much turmoil within as it did with the Montagues. They knew what I'd said was a distinct possibility.

I concentrated on two of the men who showed faint signs of a guilt they were trying to repress. Yes, they *had* seen it, they'd seen Freddi disguised as a Capulet hovering over Tybalt. They had not seen her quick work with the dagger, but they knew she must have been the one. "You two!" I pointed at them. "You know I speak the truth!"

The men gasped, appalled. A space was cleared around them, as if I'd accused them of being the murderers. Lord Capulet slowly turned, but his bulging eyes took in not just those two profusely sweating men but all of them, their silence and unease. *The powerful*, I recalled someone saying—was it Freddi? No, something I had once read, but certainly sounded like something my cousin would say—*fear only one thing, but that fear is so great it renders them completely vulnerable.* So it was here, my uncle's greatest fear materializing: he was losing power. The great Capulet family was being torn apart from the inside—and the rends had already been there, even before Freddi had slain Tybalt. And how did you fight chaos without creating more of it?

The uncomfortable lull was broken by murmurs from the guests, which escalated into excited chatter. Distinctly under the voices I heard the sound of marching feet—many of them, and as they got closer they were accompanied by angry shouts. It was the Montagues—*all* of them, it seemed, all in Montague blue-and-silver garb and all heavily armed, led by a red-faced, sword-waving Lord Montague himself. Had they followed the Capulet cavalcade in hopes of an all-out war? I had expected perhaps a couple of blood-lusty youths, the kind who liked picking fights, but certainly not the head of the great house himself.

"Oh this could be bad," Freddi muttered to me. Yet she and the party guests alike seemed more intrigued than worried. That was probably a good thing as far as the guests were concerned—they weren't panicking—but I needed Freddi to be prepared for anything.

I had never seen Lord Montague up close before—he, the head of my family's great enemy—and I was surprised to see how restrained his actions were. He glanced at Lord Capulet, who refused to meet his eyes, instead continuing to look over his oddly subdued men with increasing agitation. Seeing that the Capulets were not about to launch into another bloody brawl, Lord Montague addressed his son with stoical calmness.

"Romeo. I learned of your innocence from Friar Lawrence. The news gladdens me. I have come to bring you home." He lifted an arm almost mechanically as he spoke and gestured at his son.

Romeo drew his arm around Juliet and faced his father with fierce defiance. "Did the friar also tell you how he wed us in the church? I would rather be a servant than a lord so long as I have my wife by my side."

A figure in a flowy black silk gown darted forward. "Yes, so lovely, I, Signora Nera, am deeply honored you wish to continue to serve our house," she interjected. "But *really*, dear boy. Do not decide impetuously. Blood is undeniable. Family is irreplaceable." At that, she turned to smile at another black-dressed woman.

The woman tore off her mask, her eyes wide and her mouth gaping. "How did you know I was here?"

Nera put an arm around the woman's shoulder. "You *are* family, my dear Bianca. Of course I knew. You are my blood."

Bianca looked stunned, almost comically so. Clearly she had not been expecting such an affectionate statement. And then Nera added, "So, Sister, I am fairly certain I've won this round. You've seen it with your own eyes: sword fighting and magic certainly beat cold fish in cream sauce." She widened her smile at Bianca before turning to wink at the man behind her.

The man, Signor Petruchio, roared with laughter and kissed his wife. Thunderous applause and lusty cheers broke out from the guests. Stunned Bianca quickly became infuriated Bianca, flouncing off in a huff.

Lord Montague heard none of this, his eyes locked pleadingly with his son's. "Romeo, please. Your mother is not well—she took ill the moment you left Verona and may yet perish. Please return with me, and she may gain the strength to recover. I have spoken with Prince Escalus and he will likely lift your sentence, especially now that your innocence is proven. Please, my son." He then turned to Juliet with a kind look. "And please, my daughter. You are welcome in our house."

Now Romeo looked astonished, and skeptical, and I couldn't help feeling irked with him all over. Typical: his dream was coming true before his eyes and his only reaction was to make it more complicated. "I know you desire to give my cousin every luxury," I interjected, trying to keep testiness, sarcasm, and a number of other negative qualities from my voice, "such is your love. Therefore, accept. Your strife has ended." *Really, it has*, I thought, glaring at him. "The blood feud is over, and it is time to go home."

Juliet smiled gratefully at me, and I felt a tremendous relief that I'd never told her anything about Romeo's infatuation with me before he'd set his eyes on her. He could tell her if he chose, though there was, in my opinion, no reason why he should. She really was his first love, his true love, she who now looked adoringly at him. He returned the look and told his father, "We accept your gracious hospitality."

Lord Montague's eyes glistened—could the great and reserved man be in tears? He seemed to realize this was the case, and, straightening his stance, said with a little more authority, "If you had considered your actions more carefully, Romeo, you would have realized we never prohibited this union. If you had told us about it, we would have honored the bonds of marriage and welcomed you both immediately."

Which was very easy to say in hindsight, I thought wryly as I watched them speak together of their future at the House of Montague, but it occurred to me that he spoke the truth. Neither Juliet nor I had ever been forbidden outright from associating with the Montagues or being courted by its young men; it had been taken for granted that we would do as our elders did and hate them as enemies—and in fact, until recent events, we had done just that. I suspected the same was true for Romeo regarding the Capulets.

These thoughts fairly stunned me. This Lord Montague seemed like a reasonable man, much to my surprise. If Romeo had announced his love for Juliet—certainly if he'd announced his marriage to her—perhaps all of this would have been avoided.

But no, that was unlikely. We had all grown up steeped in hate. When love dared to intervene, it stood no chance out in the open. My cousin and Romeo, the nurse, even the friar, had all assumed the worst because what else could they do? It was like Freddi, I realized, who believed she had nothing but vengeance left to hope for until she learned to love. And even then the desire for revenge had remained stronger until now. It was always so easy to wreck things, I thought.

"Stop."

Lady Capulet's voice, like a steel blade, cut through the room, and then her person followed. She, apparently, still wanted to wreck things.

Vittoria

ALL MY LIFE, I was everything they wanted me to be, did everything I was supposed to do. I was beautiful and virtuous; I secured a rich, powerful husband; I gave him a child. Naturally, my lord wanted a son, but he was less disappointed with a daughter than many men would be. I'll say that much in his favor. I will also say that I suspect he did not like the idea of a son who would someday be stronger than he was and usurp his position as head of the Capulets. A daughter would never do that; she would be his to show off, when I, his wife, had lost my bloom. She would be his to control, in other words, just like he controlled me. He was always so jovial, so joyful, when he was in command, when those around him fell in line.

In obeying him, in giving him a daughter, I very nearly lost my life. Perhaps that was the one thing I didn't do: die honorably serving his needs. Perhaps that disappointed him. It certainly disappointed me. For weeks, months, I wanted to be dead. It felt like they'd torn me to tatters getting her out of me, and with her went every possibility of a moment free of suffering.

It disgusted me that she came from my body. I could not stand the sight of her; it was like being shown a handful of my own teeth or some repulsive growth removed from my skin. I knew those were wicked thoughts, but I felt them deep in my bones. They had removed this thing from me, this slimy, mottled, squirming *thing*, and now I only wished it removed completely.

Somehow, I got my wish.

When I recovered—but did I ever truly recover?—they put a baby back in my arms, and this one was healthy and pretty and smiling serenely at me, like a beautiful little doll. Just like that, things were different. I thought, *Yes, this is my child. It's all right now.*

Of course, I knew Nurse had a baby, too. But it was her fifth, or sixth, or seventh—I had no idea, the number seemed to change every time she brought it up, either because there was in fact another one or because she liked to embellish. In any case, it was easy for her. Have one, lose another, what did it matter to her—or to me?

In those early days I imagined strange things that seemed completely plausible—so plausible they became my reality. I thought I must have chosen a path. The other path, with the other baby, was the wrong one, where things went bad. I had avoided that fate, and all would be well.

All was well, indeed, for thirteen years, until the time came for her to step into her own predestined future.

My magnanimous husband made it seem like it would be her choice. Of course that was nonsense. He just wanted to toy with Count Paris, to place him firmly in the role of supplicant.

The count's confident, assertive nature ruffled his feathers, and he could not have that. Juliet, everyone knew, would never go against his wishes, so it was subtly demeaning to the count to suggest that a thirteen-year-old girl had the ultimate power over his future.

Thus her outburst—stridently and stubbornly refusing the count—shocked me to the core, and for a moment I thought, *How could this be my daughter?* I had brought her up to be, as I was, demure, reserved, restrained. Headstrong? Willful? How could this happen? Even then, though, my mind blotted out the thought that this was in fact *not* my daughter. Until then she had seemed to be an exact copy of myself.

I briefly considered that she might have been in love with Tybalt—hadn't I felt foolish attachments at her age? Didn't I occasionally feel them now, only to smother them right away? But I quickly rejected that possibility. Her behavior around her cousin was exactly as it should have been: polite, timid, even a little fearful. Tybalt's rage put everyone on edge, even my husband. As for Tybalt, he could never have seduced Juliet behind our backs. He had no talent for discretion and no patience for the polite and timid. He was dead and was being mourned only as much as was proper, by everyone, including Juliet. There had to be some other reason for her adamant refusal of the count.

Dimly I thought it must have been my fault somehow. If only I had made it clearer: marrying Paris was the best of all possible worlds for her. He was wealthy and titled and highly respected. It did not matter that she felt nothing for him—no, in fact, it was a huge benefit. She would not mind when he tired of her and brought others to his bed; indeed, she would be relieved. So she would never know true passion—so what? She would live in contentment, which was more than most people ever got.

Instead she chose not to live at all. Once again, my daughter was torn from me. I thought, *Yes, it is my fault: I chose a path and it was the wrong one all along. Things went bad because of it.*

This, too, was foolish. I never had any choice.

Perhaps that was why, when I found out she was alive and in love and *married* to her lover, the first thing I felt was rage. Not because of her deception, certainly not because she'd married a Montague—what did I care about that ridiculous feud?—but because she had chosen her own path and it was so vastly different from my own. No, it could not happen. I would not allow it.

Only men think they can reverse fate, and by thinking this way they bring it about. Women know better, and so we adapt. Even as I spoke, even as I tried to block her path, I knew better. Even before I saw *her*.

I recognized her, the other one, the way you do when you see people in dreams. They aren't real people you know, but they seem familiar nonetheless. She was from the other life, the one I'd thought I avoided. As she approached, for a moment I imagined that she represented a third path—the *son* I was supposed to give my lord, since she was dressed as a boy. She looked so very strong. Even had she been dressed in a fine velvet gown, there would have been no way to hide her proud stare and powerful stride. How had *this* happened? She was not like me either.

Seeing both of them there, looking at me, I wondered what they saw. Looking at them, I saw that one of them got love and the other got power. What did I get? Was it what I wanted? *What am I?*

Surely it was too late for me to ask such questions. Surely I should never ask such questions at all, nor should they; we should be links in a chain, one link to the next, binding us all together. The idea that we might not consent to such an arrangement was irrelevant. Consent did not matter where there was no choice.

Like a figure in a dream, my daughter approached.

Freddi

MY MOTHER SPOKE: "We do not consent."

She must have implied her husband in this, but it sounded more like a royal "we," given that her lord was too distraught about his own misfortunes to care much about anything else—and given that my mother was still my mother, icily haughty to the last. Everyone had turned to look at her, but I was the one who stepped before her.

"The House of Capulet is in turmoil," I pointed out calmly. "Would you have her return to such a place?"

That, I reflected, was a good question to ask myself. Why had I returned? Revenge, on these pathetic creatures? At that moment they looked like naughty children, my mother and father, rather than stately heads of a great house. I suddenly, unaccountably, felt impatient with them. They were wasting my time, and I wanted to be done and gone from them forever.

My mother's countenance fell just a little, just

enough for me to glimpse, and her voice wavered. "I cannot let her go again."

She was not looking at me when she said this, but nor was she looking at Juliet. Her eyes were unfocused, and I knew without having any of Lumi's tricks that she was thinking of one particular day long ago. "You can," I said. "Because she is not really yours, you can."

I spoke quietly so no one else was likely to hear or understand. Still not looking at me, she said, "And she who *is* my daughter?"

I don't know when or how she figured it out, but she had somehow. Perhaps she had suspected long ago, catching glimpses of me in my servant's role, only knowing for certain at this moment. Not that it mattered to me. "She was never yours either," I said. Now she met my eyes. The words might have seemed cruel to her, but in her silence and steady gaze, she seemed to acknowledge the truth of it.

Before I could stop myself, I added, "No one else need ever know," and finally she closed her eyes and nodded once.

I wanted to be uncharitable and think that of course the only thing she cared about was her own good name, that and keeping her treachery a secret from her lord and master. No one must know that she gave away her own child, no one must gossip about what a monstrous mother she was. She prized her dignity above everything else, it seemed. But the truth was I didn't want anyone else to know either. I realized we were not so unalike, she and I, both forced into a life of subservience at far too young an age. Her pains might have been insignificant compared to mine, yet I would not have traded places with her for the world.

I turned away from her at the same instant she turned from

me, and that twinned action seemed the epitome of our entire relationship. Did I get my revenge? I suppose one could see it that way, but I knew what I really had gotten was far more valuable: my freedom.

Ahead of me, I saw Lumi talking in hushed tones to Juliet, who let out a little cry and clasped both hands over her mouth. They both looked over at me. Lumi seemed uncertain, as though she wasn't sure whether to look contrite or defiant. She needn't have been either of these. I knew what she'd been saying, and given my newfound freedom, I approved.

Juliet came racing over to me. "Oh, Susan!" Her weeping now joyous, she threw her arms around me. "For so many years I wished you had lived so that you and I could grow up together. And here you are! Oh!" she added, pulling back and smiling through her tears at me. "I am so glad you were able to see Nurse—your mother—once more. What a comfort you must have been to her in her last hours."

I was—but not in the way you'll ever know. I merely nodded over her shoulder, staring straight at Lumi.

Lumi

TOO MUCH HAD happened for us to be anything but quiet and still in the carriage back to La Fortezza, and that's exactly how we were for a while. Yet there were still things I needed to say to Freddi, though I approached them with caution.

"I overheard some interesting gossip at that Black Party," I said casually. "It seems we needn't worry about Paris trying to find Juliet once he discovers that she lives. He is already wooing—and likely will be accepted by—a wealthy Milanese girl."

It occurred to me too late that this was probably not the best opening to conversation, as I'd forgotten Freddi's attraction to Paris. However, "Lucky her," was all she snorted.

I might as well come out with it. "I hope you are not upset that I told her you were Susan. I had to tell her something, as she and the others were wondering who her rescuer was."

"You should know by now I do ══════

not 'upset' that easily. Besides, it was pretty much what I had planned on saying anyway." Freddi stared out the coach window though there was nothing to see in the night outside. "I told Lady Capulet I would not reveal her secret. I did it as much for my sake as for hers. Who would want to be associated with that 'great' house now?"

She half-smirked but I sensed no real mirth in it. I noted, too, that she had referred to her mother as Lady Capulet this time—and probably for all future time. "Well, it helped Juliet, in any case. I do not know what would have happened if the truth were revealed. She would have been absolutely shocked, of course, though possibly nothing would have changed with Romeo. The boy is an impulsive imbecile, but he's no snob." Upon reflection, I snorted. "If anything he might have enjoyed the revelation. Things worked out too easily for him, I fancy."

She turned to me and the look on her face was one I'd never seen there before. I wasn't even sure what I was seeing now. She looked as exhausted as I felt, but there was something else. Could it have been… quiet satisfaction?

"Things never work out easily," she said at last, "but at least sometimes they do work out."

Syra was not angry. Nor did she seem particularly pleased, for that matter, the way she might have at least a little if we'd passed another test. As we told her what happened at the Black Party, the three of us crammed in my humble little hut (and I suppose it really was *mine* now), she listened without comment. When both Freddi and I had said everything we thought needed to be said, there was silence for a good minute or two. Then three or four.

After five threatened to pass, I gave up waiting. "So, is our work satisfactory?"

Syra nodded. "It is. Now you are ready for your first assignment."

Confusion marred what should have been a moment of joy. "You mean, for school? We're both in? When do we actually start?"

And then, as if answering something very ordinary like "How many horses are in the paddock?" or "Where is the nearest well for fresh water?" Syra said, "There is no school. There are only the two of you, and myself."

She might as well have begun babbling like a baby or crowing like a cockerel for all that I comprehended her words. How could there be no school? We were *here*. It existed, right before my eyes.

"Oh, La Fortezza is real, of course," she said, a touch impatiently, "and the nuns do study the magic of the plants. But they go no further, nor do they expect to. They know just as little about my true purpose here as you do. No longer, however. I have been looking for someone who can do what I need to be done, and I have chosen you two. I will tell you my purpose—because it's yours now as well."

PART IV

Syra

— ✳ —

MY NAME USED to be Sycorax. Yes, I know: it's the name of a witch, or so you were told as children. I was given a witch's name on purpose, so that I could show the world what witches really are. I will spare you the stories from the early parts of my life; suffice it to say I come from a long line of people who study magic, the men openly, the women secretly. This was always how it was done, even if the women were frequently much more skilled than the men, and if the secret got out, the women were called witches. Only by joining places like La Fortezza could we coexist, if tenuously, with the world.

I have a son, Caliban. I named him after his home, an island few have ever seen, a beautiful, secret place—a magical place, I daresay. My son has been enslaved by a powerful magician named Prospero. I need you to free Caliban, and it must happen immediately.

Caliban lives on this island alone. There were once others living there, of course, but they all left many years ago because of a prophecy: it would be the end of their race if they stayed. Only a prophecy that dire could make them leave their cherished home, and it had been affirmed by Caliban's father himself. Bored and curious, he had, as a young man, gone out into the world beyond the island. He crafted a boat with his own hands, sailed to the far shores of the sea, barely survived the voyage. He traveled to many places and came back with stories of beings pale as the newly dead, who killed everything they touched and remade it the way they chose. And they were coming, he warned. They had gone everywhere; it was only a matter of time before they came here.

He also came back with a baby, his child with one of those dead-pale beings. She was a witch, she had told him, surprised and intrigued that this did not scare him away. He was the first person she'd met who did not think witches were evil, and she, in turn, was the first of her kind not repelled by the "strangeness" of his hair, skin, body, and voice. They met one moonless night in Algiers, a witch-girl and an island-boy, a chance meeting when both felt a yearning for something just out of reach, and, reaching for it anyway, touched each other. This was the result, their child—*our* child.

When the islanders were about to leave for a new island home, they refused to take Caliban with them. He was half dead-pale, they said, and the dead-pale beings might come looking for him, thus fulfilling the prophecy. So Caliban's father remained, too, to care for Caliban alone on the island.

When Caliban's father took our son, I left Algiers—everyone knew about me, so I could not stay—and came to Verona. I know what you're wondering: how could I give my baby up? Or perhaps you don't wonder it at all. What place is there for an unwed rumored witch-mother of a half-breed child, after all?

This, by the way, is one reason your good Friar Lawrence distrusts me. He heard the rumors. He tried to get me to confess, to repent, tried to offer absolution. He thought he was being compassionate. I wanted none of it. I refused to be ashamed.

Caliban's father died only two years into the boy's life. He was now alone on the island. I could watch over him from afar using my magic—he could even see an image of me and hear me speak—but I could not actually be there with him. His father had asked me to stay away from the island, as he believed the appearance of one of *us* would soon bring others (and in this he was right). As it turned out, watching over Caliban was enough. The island became his mother and father. The land gave him abundant fruits, the sea provided fish, natural caves sheltered him and the water that flowed in them was sweet. He was wild and happy, and no boy could have had a better life had he been born in a palace with a hundred servants to wait on him.

And then the prophecy began to come true.

A man named Prospero and his young daughter Miranda sailed to the island. They were Neapolitan, exiled forcibly from Naples, put in a boat with a few meager supplies and sent away. Prospero had been cheated out of becoming Duke of Milan by his conniving brother Antonio, who had persuaded King Alonso of Naples to bestow the Dukedom wrongly upon Antonio himself. Do not feel too sorry for Prospero. He was a sorcerer, amateur at best in his early life but upon the island, with nothing to do but seethe at his loss and study magic, he became powerful—and, steeped in resentment for years, cruel.

Yes, he was the one who enslaved Caliban, thinking he was a threat to his Miranda. The boy was no threat. He saw someone about his age and thought that she could be his friend, that they could play together. He didn't speak their language—he spoke almost no language at all, other than to make the sounds of birds and beasts, the only "words" he knew—so Prospero could not know that the boy meant no harm when he grabbed Miranda's hand one day and pulled her across the beach into the trees. Enraged, Prospero ripped the boy away from her with a gust of wind, twirled vines around his body and bound him to a rock. Caliban was confused—were they playing with him? His confusion turned to fear as a sudden dark cloud appeared above him and poured rain. Rocks and twigs pelted his body. The island seemed angry. What had he done?

I had been watching, aghast, and I had to stop it. I shielded my boy, waved away the cloud, hissed into Prospero's ear, *Do not harm him or I will destroy you and your child.* That was a mistake. If I had threatened just him, he might have stopped, or at least desisted for a moment. But because I mentioned his daughter, he turned his rage and his powers on me.

I know your name: Sycorax, the witch. I have studied your magic and I know it better than you do. You will never come to this island again, neither yourself nor your magic. You may watch your half-breed bastard all you wish but your powers on this island are limited to that. You are helpless. How does it feel?

I do not know why he took out his need for vengeance on me, when all I had done was defend my child, just as he was doing. Nevertheless, what he said became true: I could only watch the island; I could not go there or work magic there, and I was powerless to help my boy.

Caliban and I were not the only ones to suffer from Prospero's vengeful wrath. The island, as I said, was full of magic, and that includes magical beings, or at least it had such beings before Prospero took it over. I know this is the part of my story you will find most impossible to believe; nevertheless, these things do exist. Most of them simply went about their business like the other creatures did—gathering nectar and dew to consume, singing songs, lying in the sunshine, then moving on to other places once they tired of this one. They did no harm to Caliban and he enjoyed their presence, however intangible. One, however, an airy spirit named Ariel, was not so benign. This Ariel used to play tricks on Caliban, throwing pebbles at him from different directions, or whispering in one ear and then the next, to watch the boy spin around trying in vain to figure out who or what was tormenting him, only to find nothing there. I am sure the horrid thing considered this a harmless amusement, but the boy's only friend was the island; for him to believe the island had turned on him was tragic, in my view. I used my magic to catch Ariel and trap him in a tree, where he could do no more harm to my boy. It was more than that wicked sprite deserved; there are far worse fates than to be part of a tree, to be nourished by earth and water and sunlight. No doubt a spirit of the air would find it degrading, but that was just what he needed, so that he might learn some empathy for land dwellers.

He never got enough time to learn that lesson. Soon after that, Prospero arrived, found him, and released him—only to enslave him as well.

To these two, Ariel and Caliban, he tells poisonous things about me: that I consorted with the devil and Caliban was the result, that Caliban is inherently evil because of this and deserves his bondage. Ariel believes them, of course, but my proud, magnificent boy does not. He rages at his captor—in Prospero's own language, which had been forced upon him because his own beautiful words were deemed savage—and defends his father and me, even though Prospero told him that, like his father, I was long dead.

All of this was mere child's play to Prospero; he had bigger plans. He has been waiting for a chance to get back at his enemies, and that chance is coming. Those who took away Prospero's kingdom will soon be going close to the island, having no idea that he's there and no clue of the revenge he's planning. I do not care what happens to any of the rest of them—that is not my concern in the least. But Prospero does not care what innocents he takes down in the process of getting even with his enemies. He cares deeply for his own child and would never do anything to harm her, but still he would use her as a pawn in his game. He despises my son and would not hesitate to harm him. I cannot let that happen; my son must be saved. This is your task. Complete it and you will then be free to go anywhere you desire.

Lumi

M Y MIND WHIRLED. I could not get hold of anything solid to steady myself, so I glanced at Freddi to see her reaction. She was rapt, eyes wide, leaning forward, no trace of her usual sneering skepticism. I supposed a story about an unfairly enslaved child would get her attention like nothing else could. I supposed, when it came to that, it should probably get anyone's attention, but Freddi could identify with this Caliban more than most. That made me wonder, though, how much truth there was to Syra's story—or, rather, whether the events of it could be viewed another way, and what parts she had omitted. Syra had already been withholding a lot from us. There was no school; she had made everyone—Friar Lawrence, Grigio, the rest of La Fortezza, and Freddi and me—think there was so that she could pursue her own agenda. How much could we trust her?

I knew, of course, that she'd be reading these thoughts—I wasn't bothering to hide them—so there was no point in pretending I wasn't hesitant or doubtful. "Syra," I said, "you are infinitely more powerful than the _____ two of us combined. I imagine this Prospero is likewise. Why would you want *us* to do something so important and difficult? We weren't even capable of figuring out that there was no magic school and that you had deceived us," I couldn't help adding.

Syra nodded, clearly having anticipated the question and clearly ignoring the final remark. "Prospero *is* powerful. He knows it, too, which is precisely his weakness. He thinks he is more powerful than anyone he has ever known, and he aims to show it. But he won't waste such a show on anyone he believes to be vastly inferior to himself and irrelevant to his goals. He has a daughter, about your age, whom he controls completely. He would likely think he can do the same with you."

"He would be right. But according to you, because he *can* control us, he won't *bother* to control us?" *How does that make sense*, I didn't need to add. I was frustrated that Syra refused to admit any wrongdoing, and I felt used, cheated—wronged.

Syra continued smoothly, "Does a hunter pursue a mouse? He won't get much from eating it, and it can't do him much harm, so it would be a waste of his time to go after something so small and inconsequential."

I shrugged off the insulting comparison to rodents and asked, "But what can a mouse possibly get from him?"

"Anything she wants." It was Freddi. "If the mouse is bold and not timid, if she thinks and acts carefully instead of panicking, she can make his life hell and he would never know the cause."

She and Syra had locked eyes in a way that made me uneasy. "I thought our purpose was to rescue Caliban, not to 'make Prospero's life hell'," I interjected.

One corner of Freddi's lips tilted upward, and I swear I could see that cool half-smile reflected in Syra as well. "Who says you can't have more than one goal?"

Now I was truly alarmed. Whatever happened to "only do good"? I knew reminding them of that would not be the right way to approach this, but I was at a loss as to what the right way might be. "How are we supposed to achieve these 'more than one' goals?" I took a breath and went on. "Prospero defeated *you*, Syra, and all the magic Freddi and I know could fit in your little finger. This makes our fight at the Black Party look like a fair one. We are absurdly overmatched. Not to mention we know nothing about this island—I've never been outside Verona other than that single trip to Padua." Now I paused. "We need a plan."

This was a risk. I figured being adversarial would get me nowhere, so perhaps if we actually started looking realistically at the situation, they might admit how utterly impossible it all was. Or I might be stuck trying to do something utterly impossible.

"Yes, you do," said Syra, not missing a beat. "And I cannot help you much with that. The more involved I am, the more likely Prospero will divine what is happening and put a stop to it."

Wonderful. Now we were stuck doing something impossible with minimal assistance.

"I can get us to Naples," Freddi said, excitement ringing in her voice and flashing in her eyes. "And from there passage on a boat. I learned a lot from other servants who had husbands who traveled—the best routes, decent inns, what to avoid. Once we find the island—"

"Which we'll do—how, exactly?"

Syra actually waved a dismissive hand at that question. Waved her hand! As if I'd asked what kind of hats we should wear. "That will not be a problem. The island will find you."

Now even Freddi looked perplexed. She had little use, it seemed, for magic metaphors.

Syra turned to her. "Fiamma Fredda, you said you overheard 'all kinds of gossip' at the Black Party. Did you hear anything about the King of Naples, perchance?"

Still bewildered, Freddi said, "I believe there was talk about his daughter's impending wedding to a member of the royal family of Tunis." She snorted. "Everyone talked as if they'd known the couple since birth, acting like of course *they* had been invited but simply could *not* find the time to travel to *Africa* just now."

"'Just now' is correct. The wedding is within a fortnight. King Alonso, Princess Claribel, and their entourage set sail for Tunis in four days. The one thing I can tell you—one thing that is crucial—is that you need to be on their ship." Syra moved a few steps away, looking off into the distance as if she could see hundreds of miles away. Perhaps she could. "Prospero will not miss this chance—it's the one he's been waiting for. If you are on that ship, as I said, the island will find you."

"Well, all right then. That simplifies things," I said. It was stupid to be sarcastic, but this thing was becoming more ridiculous by the minute.

Freddi's blank-faced silence suggested she thought the same thing. Finally she said again, "I can get us to Naples," but that was all.

Syra nodded and turned briskly to leave. "Good. I will leave you to your plans."

We watched her go; there was no point in calling her back, protesting, begging for more. We were on our own. There was no school, no teachers, no other students, just us.

∽

The beginning of our journey involved no magic but a lot of carpentry.

him without stepping out of the circle. Then he'd make it ever smaller. It was an excellent way for me to use my whole body and not just my arm." She stood. "Stand. We'll begin now."

She found a brass candle holder from among the gifts and held it up for me to see. "I'm going to try to hit you with this. You are going to stop me."

"How about 'tap,' not 'hit.' You could kill me with that if you wanted to," I said warily.

"Well, then, stop me."

She thrust the thing at my right arm. I grabbed her wrist before it could connect. My pleasure at this early success was short-lived, for I suddenly felt a sharp pain in my upper left arm. In her other hand she held the twin of the first candle holder. "That's cheating!" I exclaimed, clutching my arm. "I didn't know you were going to use both hands!"

"Why wouldn't I? This is a fight. Plus I am right-handed, of course; why would I *not* use my right hand? You weren't paying attention."

I grimaced. I could easily have stopped her with magic but I wasn't a cheater, I thought loftily. She tossed me one of the candlesticks. "Now you try to hit me with it. Meanwhile I'll keep trying to"—she smirked—"'tap' you with mine. Don't just use your arm. You've got an entire body, and if you're not using it, it's all a target and not a weapon."

It was too much all at once, and standing there on wobbly legs in a dark, cramped space with a girl who had killed at least one person (and who knows if there were more I didn't know about), I fell back on the one thing I knew would work: magic. In short, I cheated.

I shared Freddi's vision and saw immediately how I was, indeed, all target. I was so focused on the weapon in her right hand that I wasn't thinking about anything else. She could step on my feet, kick my shins, jab her knee into my torso. She could even hit me with her head, or turn slightly and ram her shoulder into me with all her weight.

I released myself from her view and tried to read from her stance which of these she might attempt. But she was moving too fast, too deceptively, so I panicked and magically froze the arm with the candlestick.

I tapped her on the forehead with the tip of my weapon.

It should have been a hilarious victory on my part, but only Freddi grinned; I merely lowered my candlestick and sat down with a sigh. "Yes, I cheated," I muttered. "I couldn't think what else to do."

"Why so glum about it? It worked. You won."

"I haven't learned anything new. I already know that kind of magic. I still don't know how to fight."

Freddi shrugged and sat down too. "Take any advantage you can. That's lesson number one."

Unconvinced, I studied the intricate, swirling design on the candlestick and marveled at the skill of the crafter. Then an idea struck me. "I can return the favor, Freddi. I can teach you some magic if you like." I put down the candlestick and sat up, suddenly excited. "There might be some herbs in here somewhere, but we don't actually need them. We can use the sound of the waves, the way the boat feels on those waves. These are sensations we're both having right now. All right: I'm going to think of a happy memory from my childhood, and you try to figure out what it is."

I glanced at Freddi to see if she was with me. She had her arms crossed and a look on her face—the face one makes when one's arms are crossed. "I have no happy memories from my own childhood. I have no idea what anyone else's might be."

"Oh, right, er, sorry," I stammered, feeling insensitive, though part of me was annoyed at her lack of effort. "All right, I'm going to think of the last person who…" I had been about to ask the question I'd asked Friar Lawrence during my first foray into magic, but it occurred to me that the last person who made me angry was Freddi herself and that she could figure *that* out without magic. "… who made me feel happy."

Freddi sighed, but the look of concentration on her face suggested she was at least giving it a try. The boat rocked. Seconds went by. Freddi sighed again, this time impatiently. "Lumi, sorry, but this just isn't something I do. I don't get into people's heads. That's your area."

As if to emphasize "my area," she moved to the far side of the crate, which wasn't really very far at all, but still made her point: she and I were different.

The funny thing is, the last person who had made me feel happy was Freddi herself, when we were working together as a team at that Black Party, when I heard Nera speak of family and blood and I thought, *yes, this person is just that to me*, not just because her mother and my mother were sisters but because we shared this crucial experience. Perhaps I had been entirely mistaken and we shared nothing at all.

Being stuck in a crate with your cousin (with *my* cousin in particular) for three days would make anyone want to leap for joy once outside, but I had extra reason to. Here I was, though I still couldn't quite believe it. At the beginning of the month, I had never left Verona. And now here I was in Tunisia—in Africa! We had come to the shore of this vast, magnificent continent, and I wanted to see everything. Here in Tunis I yearned to explore the bustling marketplace, view the stunning mosques, sample the fragrant, spicy foods, all things I'd only heard about. But I knew we should stick with the wedding party; if we separated from them, we might lose them entirely, and that would mean not only not fulfilling our duty to Syra but also being stranded here. Besides, a Tunisian-Neapolitan wedding was certain to be as spectacular as anything else we might experience.

"You know we have to stay here, right?"

"Ha ha. Help me with the door," I muttered, feeling for the panel in the crate that would slide open for us to emerge. Freddi grabbed my arm.

"Lumi, we discussed this. We'll be seen if we go ashore with the wedding party, and we might get lost or otherwise detained if we go on our own. We have to fulfill Syra's mission, not play at being tourists."

I shook her arm off and stared at her as if I had the power to fling daggers with my eyes. Would that I had *that* kind of magic. "Freddi. We *are* fulfilling Syra's mission. We're here, aren't we? We can still do other things besides rescue her son, especially since we haven't reached the island yet and have no way of getting there ourselves since it's supposed to 'find us.' This is the chance of a lifetime. Are you really going to let that chance go while we just sit in a box?"

Freddi stared at me, just stared, saying nothing. This exasperated me so much I weighed the possibility of using the meager abilities I'd gained in fighting. I'd lose badly if I did, of course, but at that moment I didn't care. She was standing in the way of the thing I wanted the most. But I didn't have to fight her. I could freeze her and walk right on by. And she knew this as well as I did.

I took a deep breath. I could do what I wanted. Couldn't I?

I let the breath out and felt truly deflated. Of course I couldn't. Freddi was not the only obstacle between me and the world. The world itself was the obstacle. It was not designed with me in mind. I would be incredibly lucky if I somehow managed to do this extraordinary thing Syra wanted us to do; any more than that was impossible.

We were still and silent in the crate for several minutes. Finally, I muttered, "I guess we could continue our lessons," though without any enthusiasm. It hardly seemed to matter whether I learned to fight; it would never be enough.

Freddi shrugged, likely sensing my lack of enthusiasm. It should have been obvious even to her. But then she surprised me by saying, "Honestly, Lumi, you don't need my help with fighting. You're good at magic—really good. Good enough for both of us. As long as we're careful, we'll get by just fine." She leaned back against a wall of the crate, closed her eyes, and hummed some tune she'd picked up from the shiphands.

I knew Freddi did not dole out praise easily or often, certainly not to me. I was sensible of the compliment, but it would be so much better for us if Freddi could back me up, keeping eyes away from us, and as I listened to her humming I couldn't help but think she had not been trying hard enough on purpose. Even Friar Lawrence had been able to do some basic accessing of thoughts, and he'd said nearly everyone could do so if they knew it was possible and tried it out. Either Freddi was holding back or she was the sad exception to "nearly everyone," and while I thought the latter unlikely, I couldn't see a reason why she would hold back.

The strange thing was that I was the one who felt discouraged. Unless Freddi was hiding her frustration better than I thought she could, she seemed to accept her inability with equanimity. Perhaps she preferred the idea of fighting her way out of any danger. Stranger still was that over the next couple of days while the ship docked, and then as it returned to sea, I increasingly felt... cheated, somehow, and not just because I had missed out on seeing Tunis and the wedding. All this excitement about magic, about being able to control people's minds and bodies and all that—in the end, it was nothing more than an ordinary tool, a means to an end, like having a pleasing voice for oration. Syra had not used any kind of magic to convince us to do her bidding. Likewise, Prospero may have been powerful, but so far as I could tell, he was using those powers to enslave others (which could easily be done without magic, as even my sketchy knowledge of history proved) and to enact revenge (which was something even a girl like Freddi with no power save brute force could do).

Added to that was, of course, the irony that the sole purpose of my magic right now was not to throw thunderbolts or levitate things or anything else showy and awe-inspiring, but rather the opposite: to make us unnoticed. The hold was now a lot emptier than it had been on the outbound journey, and none of it was off limits anymore, so the crew could come and go much more easily, looking through the barrels and boxes and crates for whatever they might need. That meant constant vigilance on our part; if anyone came down here, we'd have to be silent and still, and if someone approached our crate, I would have to divert their attention to something else. *That* meant constant focus on my part, and it was wearing me down. The sea had been calm on the outgoing voyage, its gentle motion barely noticeable down in the hold. The waters were raging now, the ship tossed like an ill-built child's toy, and even the most hardened sailors aboard were struggling.

But the choice was no choice: I could feel wretched, or we could be discovered. It was, therefore, almost a relief to me when two days later the storm finally hit.

Freddi

WHEN THE STORM hit, I had been moments away from apologizing to Lumi. Thank goodness for timing and tempests.

I admit, I felt bad: she was, so far, doing nearly all of the hard work and suffering mightily for it. But what could I do? I was not adept at magic, not like she was. I couldn't help her keep us hidden. So I let her work, keeping quiet while also keeping my ears open to pick up any useful information. The crate had been placed near the door, and I could sometimes hear people passing by on the deck. I rarely heard anything important or even interesting. The night of the storm, however, I heard something amazing.

I had convinced Lumi we were safe enough at night that she could rest completely, so she was deep in an exhausted sleep when I heard the song. Someone was humming a lovely, complex tune just outside the doorway down to the hold. They must have seated themselves there, for the song continued without waning for some time. After so many days of hearing nothing but my cousin's voice and my own, interrupted occasionally by the mariners' cusses and the royal entourage's lofty babble, this was a feast for my ears.

I had to hear more. Slowly, silently, I left the crate and climbed above deck.

It was Prince Ferdinand. He was seated on a box with a barrel before him, a chess game on the barrel. He studied the game for a moment, then moved for the white side, still humming. Then, sensing my presence, he looked up.

I had not slipped up; I had wanted him to see me. I was starved for the company of someone other than my cousin, and here was not just a meal but a feast. The prince was a strikingly handsome young man, and I was not going to pass up the chance to at least say a word or two.

"Evening, sir," I said casually. "What's that you're humming, may I ask?"

"It's a Tunisian melody. I heard it at the royal wedding and I can't get it out of my mind, though I don't know any of the words." His voice itself was musical, and I hoped he'd say more. "I am sorry if I disturbed you."

"It beats hearing the same old sea shanties night after night," I said, and he laughed.

"You must have a lot of good stories to tell. Most mariners do."

"I wasn't always a sailor," I said, thinking quickly. "Before this I worked in a great house as a servant." All true, so far. "I have stories from *there*, but I ought not tell them to Your Royal Highness. You will wonder what your own servants are getting up to."

He laughed again, and I was so entranced by his smile and

his eyes, a dove-gray color I could discern even in the low light, that I almost missed what he said. "I have not seen you before on this vessel."

"Usually I'm below deck," I said, trying to think of some kind of explanation for why I was here now. I decided not to explain. Deception, I knew, worked best when you gave away as little as possible.

"Ah, well, you picked a good time to be above. The winds have blown the night sky free of clouds, and the heavens are clear to see."

He gestured to the stars, but my eyes remained fixed on him for a moment. *Yes, the heavens are clear to see*, I thought, before tearing my gaze away from him.

The stars were indeed bright, and I tried to remember some of the names of the constellations I'd learned from one of the nuns who knew astronomy. "The bears," I murmured, pointing them out, "big and little."

"That's right!" he exclaimed. I worried suddenly that he might ask me what some of the others were—as a sailor, I probably should have known them all. "I know there's a story that explains why their tails are so long, but I can't recall it just now."

Thankfully I did know this one. "The big bear was a woman who was turned into a bear, then whirled around and flung into the sky by her tail—for her protection, I believe." That part had always seemed absurd to me, more so than the flinging part. She was a *bear*. She could protect herself. "The small bear was her son, also turned into a bear and flung the same way so that he could be with her. That is why their tails are so long."

He beamed at me. "I had forgotten that wonderful story!" He gazed appreciatively once more at the stars, and then I thought his eyes saddened. "How lovely to get to see his mother there always. It has been ten years since my mother's passing. And now dear Claribel will be living far from us. Without women around to make life bearable, men are pathetic creatures indeed, and such will be my father and I." He laughed ruefully.

I would have given anything to comfort him at that moment. "Your sister, the princess, she is happy?"

"Yes, I believe so. Her husband is an excellent man, and she loves the Tunisian people and their land. She is already quite fluent in the language—Claribel has a gift for learning languages." His pride in her was obvious. "It is a great comfort to my father and myself to know that though she will be far from us, she will have a good life with a good man." He turned to me with a smile. "Were you able to see Tunis at all while we stopped?"

I shook my head, and to my great delight (and slight guilt as I pictured Lumi back at the crate, exhausted from doing magic and disappointed at missing Tunis), he told me about the city we'd just left—the souks, the medina, the ruins of Carthage. "The streets smell of saffron, jasmine, and the sea. If you ever get back, I recommend getting out and just wandering. I couldn't do much of that—the royal family does *not* simply *wander*." He grinned, and I had the feeling an older relative must have said that to him and his sister endlessly when they were children. "But if you have leave, you should enjoy your freedom to roam."

I wanted to stay there all night, but I needed to hasten back to the crate before Lumi noticed my absence, if she hadn't already. "Well, back belowdecks with me," I said, trying to sound like the hale-and-hearty mariner I was supposed to be. "Enjoy your chess game, but watch that black knight."

"I will! But before you go, what is your name?"

"Freddi," I said, relieved that I would not need to invent yet another fake one.

"Freddi. You know chess, I see—perhaps we could play a game sometime before we reach port."

I nodded, trying to look cool though my heart threatened to burst from my chest and splatter on the deck. "I'd like that."

Now he looked mischievous. "And if I win, I will insist you tell me stories from your servant's days."

I almost countered with what I would insist upon if *I* won, but that would have been outrageously impertinent. Instead I grinned, nodded, and departed.

As I snuck back to the hold, I tried to keep my feelings level. The prince could not be so naive as to imagine a lowly mariner could play a game of chess with a royal passenger; he was just making conversation. He did not enjoy my company— he could not possibly enjoy the company of the likes of me. And anyway, even if he had enjoyed our brief time together, I wasn't who he thought I was. Yes, all this and more I told myself sternly but I could not help it: I felt like I was flying.

The flight was a short one. The moment I'd crept back into the crate and closed the panel behind me, I met Lumi's eyes. She was sitting very straight upright and staring hard at me.

"I went up to get air," I mumbled.

"Do you usually talk to princes when you get air?" she snapped. "I heard your voices, Freddi."

"He saw me, so we talked. He's the only one who saw me, Lumi. Nobody else came by. I didn't expose us."

Lumi staggered to her feet, her arms akimbo, as if she needed to take up as much space as she could to make her point. "Every moment I've been on this miserable ship, I've felt like my body and soul are being twisted and churned and wrung like a rag. It's roasting hot in here, it stinks, and while I'm here doing everything I can to keep us from being found out, you—you go out promenading with the King's son all over the deck?"

"Not promenading and not all over the deck. We had one short conversation, that's all. No one else saw us, and he thinks I'm part of the crew."

"Oh, does he?" she hissed. "Perhaps he's seen through your disguise and realizes you're a young girl—a beautiful one, at that. Perhaps he's courting you, Freddi. Princess Freddi of Naples—that sounds lovely, doesn't it?"

I stared at her, stunned. She had divined, somehow, a little of what I was feeling for Prince Ferdinand, and was mocking me mercilessly for it. At any other time this spiteful sarcasm would have enraged me to the point of violence. But before fury could ignite in me, I saw her pale, clammy skin, her shaking hands and trembling shoulders, the unsteady sway of her whole body, and I knew I was the one in the wrong. I opened my mouth to speak but the words felt stuck in my throat.

It wouldn't have mattered if speech had come forth anyway. Just then thunder cracked and boomed, shaking the entire ship. Heavy rain crashed upon the deck, followed by a swell of waves. The tempest was here, and our antagonism fell away as we both knew we had bigger problems than staying concealed.

Lumi

I F THE VIOLENT sway of the boat and deafening din of
the storm weren't enough to convince us that we were in
peril, the shouts of the men above deck confirmed it. King
Alonso's men screamed at the sailors to do *something* to keep
them all from drowning and the shiphands screamed back at the
King's men to get the bloody hell (with a few other choice words)
out of the way so they *could* do something. Freddi and I both
knew what we had to do: get our raft ready.

"Good thing Syra planned for this," Freddi said as we
struggled to bring the hinged walls down flat.

It struck me just then that Syra might have *known* this
would happen—that this was what she'd meant by her cryp-
tic remark that the island would find us. Was the storm Prospero's doing? Did he intend to break apart the ship and kill
all those onboard? But that would mean killing a number
of innocent men as well as his enemies. Still, vengeful rage
didn't always cede to a sense of fairness.

"We're done! We just need to carry it to the deck," Freddi yelled.

"And then what?" I muttered, not expecting Freddi to hear or answer.

We got the raft on deck just in time to witness something I simply could not understand. As the ship lurched under me, I saw what looked like giant arms reaching up from the sea—as though an enormous creature made of water were climbing aboard. The liquid arms thrashed around until they found a victim—a *man*—and seized him, dragging him off the ship. Some men, I noticed, the arms passed right by, and it looked very much as though the creature was searching for specific people.

"*Father!*"

The voice was the prince's. An oceanic arm had latched onto the King and before anyone could do anything, he'd been pulled sharply away.

"Prince Ferdinand, look out!" screamed Freddi next to me. She lurched toward him but I grabbed her shoulder and held her back.

Another arm had taken the prince. A sailor batted at the arm with a heavy stick but in vain—the stick passed right through. The arm was just water.

Freddi now pulled at the raft. "Come on! We need to go after them!"

"Wait until the ship dips on this side," I yelled. "It'll be easier that way."

When the ship tilted down its port side, where we were, we launched the raft. In the tumult I half expected to drown right then and there, but surprisingly we landed without turning over. When a wave surged toward us, instead of taking us under, it merely propelled us forward. I looked back at the ship and noticed that the storm had moved away from it entirely—and that the ship looked nearly undamaged. How was that possible? Even stranger, the few damaged parts I saw were rapidly being repaired, but not by the crew.

The ship was repairing itself.

Loose boards reattached. A broken mast righted itself. And the crew members, one by one, lay down on the now-calm deck and curled up to sleep.

I gaped, but too many things were happening for me to process. I turned back to look for the prince. Freddi had been frantically scanning the choppy waters herself and suddenly motioned with her head, wisely not daring to let go with a hand to point. "There! The prince! Over there!"

We both shouted at the gasping figure, still a good many fathoms from us and looking in the wrong direction. I tried to ignore all the chaos around me and focused on being in his mind, turning his head toward us. It worked: his head jerked our way and, seeing us, he began thrashing his way toward the raft.

Meanwhile Freddi and I attempted to steer toward him, though "steering" meant little more than leaning our heads and shoulders in the direction of the prince while gripping the boards and desperately trying not to slide off. Just when a lucky surge of water brought us almost close enough for him to grab the raft, the prince froze, one arm extended toward us, as if he'd been turned into a statue. Only instead of heavy marble that sank, he seemed weightless, because his body lifted out of the water until he barely skimmed its surface. A blast of wind then swept him away, so fast he was out of sight almost before we could react.

Freddi gasped, "No," staring at the spot where Prince

Ferdinand had been. I stared as well, but then tilted my head upward. I had the strange sensation that *the storm had turned to look at us.* It felt as if a powerful force was studying us, *curious* about us. For a moment it hovered there and then I felt it—something—reaching down to us. In the next moment we too were hurled forward after Ferdinand, flung at breathtaking speed across the water toward, I could only guess, the island.

How beautiful. That was my first thought when I looked up from the sand. More intensely bizarre things had happened in the last few days than I ever imagined possible, so it was very near astonishing that despite the whirlwind of my head, I could still look up and admire the scenery.

Every sight, sound, and smell seemed twice as intense here. The sand, shimmering gold, sifted like sugar in my hands—I wanted to scoop up a handful and eat it, as I'd only tasted sugar once in my life, at a party at my uncle Capulet's, of course. Bold-hued flowers dotted nearby foliage, their fragrance harmonizing with the salty sea air. Was there ever a bluer sky, greener leaves? Could any trees bear more luscious fruit than these? I wanted to breathe it all in, taste it, run into those trees and melt into the island.

I tried to stand up and fell over. Maybe not just yet.

Next to me, Freddi had already sat up and was scanning up and down the beach anxiously. Of course: she was looking for the prince. *Don't worry about me. I'm fine,* I thought sourly, but began looking in the opposite direction for any signs of human life. Prospero would have wanted the King and the prince, his brother Antonio, and probably a few others in the King's entourage—maybe all of them.

I straightened. "There!" I whispered. Freddi whipped her head around and I pointed at a bedraggled figure who staggered up the beach and lay down under a shady tree. Freddi bolted to her feet but I grabbed her ankles and held her in place. "Stop. He's fine, Freddi. Just let him rest. We need to start planning what we're going to do."

She scowled at me but sat down again, positioning herself so that she could keep an eye on Ferdinand.

I told her what I had seen before we'd been brought here: the ship repairing itself, the men on deck lying down and going to sleep, and the storm seeming to have a mind. "It's all Prospero's doing, obviously. At least he didn't destroy the ship outright. He must have brought only those he has a grudge against, sparing the others. Perhaps they'll wake in a few hours and sail back to Naples, assuming the King and the others drowned."

"But why are *we* here?" Freddi asked. "We're not with King Alonso. And what you said about the storm suggests we were also brought here for some reason."

"I know. What in the world could that reason be? Prospero doesn't know us—unless somehow he figured out we're working for Syra. That would be very bad if true."

Freddi didn't seem all that concerned; she continued to watch Prince Ferdinand. At that moment the prince stirred a little, and I noticed something: Freddi instantly changed. The differences were subtle, but her posture, her expression, everything about her seemed to shift a little. She was slipping on her "shiphand" persona, I realized, just in case the prince should open his eyes and see her. She was good at that, I mused, putting on different guises.

I gasped. "That's it," I croaked hoarsely. "I figured it out!"

Freddi didn't even bother to turn her head, so focused was she on the prince. "What? Why we're here?"

"No," I said hastily, realizing this would seem like a complete non sequitur. I couldn't help my excitement, though, and I continued, "The kind of magic you should be doing. The reason you couldn't do the other kind. It has to draw from you, from your personality and strengths. Friar Lawrence believes in the magic the Divine Creator has bestowed on plants, so he concerns himself with that. Me? I've always wanted to see the world from other eyes, so I *do*. But that's not you. Your magic is something else." I could tell she was listening even though she pretended to barely pay heed. "Disguise yourself from me," I commanded.

Now she looked back at me, trying to feign insolence. "Will that make you leave me alone?"

"If you're hidden, I can hardly bother you." Ha, that put her in a bind. She didn't want to do what I'd asked because it was me asking, and yet I *knew* she wanted to try. "It's what you do, you see? You have always been under disguises, always hiding who you really are. That's your magic: illusions. That's why— Hey. Where did you…?"

For a moment I lost sight of her, the way a mother might lose sight of a child in a marketplace, which was incredibly strange because there was no one or nothing around her. Yet that's what it felt like: I hadn't seen her vanish but the fact remained that she was no longer there. *Something* was there, though. I stared hard at the space she'd occupied seconds ago and rubbed my eyes. It was as though there was a blind spot in the center of my vision, something gray and fuzzy and easily overlooked. I blinked again and there was Freddi, back in view.

We looked at each other, our faces mirrors of astonishment. "Did I just...?" Freddi mumbled uncertainly.

I nodded. "Yes, you did! This is wonderful!"

Slowly a grin widened across her face. "Wow. I mean, wow! It was—easy. I don't mean to brag, but—"

"Oh go ahead and brag," I chuckled. "And there's a reason it was easy. You don't know it but you've been practicing all along. All your disguises, all the time you spent trying to be inconspicuous in the House of Capulet, all that was part of your training, so to speak. It's even possible you've been doing this all along quite literally." I considered her for a moment, pondering how this discovery could help us. "Hmm. I wonder. Do you think you could hide us both?"

She considered this. "When I used to practice with Mercutio, sometimes it seemed like..." She glanced at me, and it was the look of someone wary of being made fun of. I nodded my encouragement. "Well, it seemed like I was willing the whole world to ignore us so that we could be alone together."

"Then maybe that's the way to do this?"

"Well, I'll try, though I'm not sure how we can test that." She took a few deep breaths, her face relaxing its tension, and then she looked around. A large brown-and-white bird stood on the sand a few strides away; Freddi motioned to me and we crept closer to it. The bird darted its head left and right, puzzled—it could hear us and see the sand shifting beneath our feet, but we were able to get within touching distance of it because *it could not see either of us*. Freddi released the spell and the startled bird flew off. She did the same thing several more times, surprising three more birds and a small crab. We were both giggling now. It felt immensely satisfying to have something to laugh about for a change.

"You can do this! This is wonderful!" My excitement surged—now there were two of us with magic—and then slowly faded. Yes, this was wonderful, but it was still only one small addition to the meager arsenal we had to fight Prospero.

The storm had been an astounding feat. He had made a tempest violent enough to rattle apart the ship, yet it only plucked out those on board who concerned him—the King's party, plus us by accident—leaving everyone else safe on a ship that had somehow sustained no damage. All that in a blink or two of an eye. Perhaps Syra was capable of similar things, but I had never seen it, and anyway Syra wasn't here; it was just us.

Freddi saw my frown and raised an eyebrow. "How are we going to do this?" I asked. "We've got a couple of things we can do, but Prospero is *incredibly* powerful."

"Yes, and incredibly determined to get revenge," added Freddi, now also somber.

"And all we have is the fact that nobody else knows we're here." Though even this, I reflected privately, I was not sure of. "That is our only advantage, and it's not very helpful." I sifted the sand listlessly through my fingers. "Freddi, tell me this: what made you decide not to seek revenge on the Capulets?"

For a moment she said nothing. Perhaps she still regretted that decision. Then she shrugged. "They destroyed themselves before I could get to them. That was enough—maybe even better, in fact."

I shook my head with frustration. "That doesn't help us. I don't see Prospero destroying himself unless..." I stopped. A terrible thought had entered my head and I refused to pursue it further.

"Unless we consider where he's most vulnerable," Freddi finished smoothly. "That's how it's done, after all." I looked at her, aghast. Had she finally learned the mind-reading magic too, at this, the worst possible moment?

"His daughter," she continued, picking up a pretty, whorled seashell and tossing it with one hand, thoughtfully gazing at its rising and falling. "He hates everyone in the world right now except his daughter Miranda."

"Freddi," I said with a voice that shook a little. "We are not going to harm that girl."

She looked surprised and put the shell back in the sand. "Who said anything about harming her? You really do think I'm bloodthirsty, Cousin."

She didn't seem to mind being thought of that way, though. "Well then what do you mean? What about Miranda?"

"Something that—" She hesitated, glancing at and then quickly away from the prince. "Ferdinand, something that he said about his sister and father. He was telling me about Tunis, and then suddenly he stopped like he'd just realized something and said Claribel's wedding was both the saddest and happiest day of his father's life—sad because he might never see her again, happy because it was the best thing a father could ask for a daughter: that when he could no longer protect her, he knew she could go out into the world with a good man who was trustworthy and caring."

She took a deep breath. "I'm not an idiot, Lumi. I know I could never be with someone like Prince Ferdinand. He thinks I'm a shiphand. Even if he knew who I really was it wouldn't matter. My life has been too strange for me to enter into a proper, stable marriage with anyone like that. And"—she gestured wryly at the island and her bedraggled mariner's clothing—"it continues to be strange. But what about this Miranda? She's Neapolitan, daughter of a man who rightfully should be a duke. By my calculations she's around our age—marrying age. They would be perfect for each other. What if they fell in love? Prospero might see that as the best thing for her."

"I suppose," I said without enthusiasm. "How is this supposed to solve anything?"

"Well, it wouldn't do for him to seek revenge on the father of the boy his daughter is in love with, would it? Look at what happened with Lord Montague. He ended generations of feuding when he accepted his son's Capulet bride into his home."

"Yes," I said, slowly warming to the idea. "Yes! If he can make peace with King Alonso, well, it'd be a stretch to think he could forgive his brother's treachery, but at least he would be inclined to return to Italy on his daughter's behalf. And the King would *have* to let them both come back."

"And he'd leave Caliban alone. And we'd succeed."

"Great! So… what are we supposed to do? Ferdinand is a wonderful boy, but, well, not every girl in the world is going to desire him the instant they see him." *Not every girl is* you, *in other words*, was the gross understatement I would never say to her. "There's no guarantee he and Miranda will fall in love at first sight—or at any number of sightings."

"I was thinking we could help things along."

I nodded encouragement for her to continue. So far it was a ridiculous plan, but it was something to start with. Privately, I was also relieved that Freddi was being clear-headed about the prince. I had not wanted to say anything about her admission that someone like Ferdinand could never love someone like her; that was a humiliating thing for her to have to declare, even if it had a lot of truth to it. I had always been determined that no one would love me, because that kind of love just didn't interest me, and I had made my life different from others' lives on purpose in that regard. Freddi had had no choice in the matter. Like so many other people in this sad world, she longed for the one thing she had very little chance of getting.

"All right," I said cautiously. "It's as good a plan as any, given that we haven't got anything else. Next problem: we have one half of our matchmaking subjects here, but we have no idea where Miranda is, and a whole island where she could be. How can—"

I jerked my head around, staring into the trees. I had the strong sensation—more than that, the certainty—that someone was looking at me. It was the same sensation I'd had during the storm, only this time it was coming from a clearing in the trees.

It wanted me to follow. It knew where Miranda was and would show her to me.

Freddi was looking at the same place, but did not seem to have the same impressions I did. "What is it?" she hissed.

I took a deep breath. Was I really going to do something this questionable, following a mysterious whatever-it-was into the depths of a strange island? Well, what else could I do? I turned to Freddi. "Freddi, the prince knows you. Work on him somehow, make him think he's about to meet his true love, then after a bit take him the same way I'm going. I'll mark it in a way you can follow. I'll be fine," I added, seeing how taken aback she was. "I'm going to find Miranda."

I walked toward the clearing, smiling a little to think that Freddi would have another chance to talk to her prince. The smile faded as I peered into the uncertain path before me. Well, I'd wanted adventure, and here it was.

Freddi

I WATCHED LUMI TAKE a deep breath and march into the trees. I had to admire her. I was taking a similar about-to-plunge breath, though I was facing not a mysterious island, but a man.

I got up and tried to brush some of the sand off my tunic. It stuck like sugar on the fancy pastries the Capulets sometimes had (the crumbs of which the servants greedily fought for), so I gave up trying and trudged over to Ferdinand, trying to look casual as I stumbled over the uneven ground.

"Sir! It's you!" *Well of course it is*, I thought, already feeling foolish. "Prince Ferdinand, it's Freddi from the ship." *Where else would I be from?* "Are you all right, sir?"

The prince turned, sat up, and looked at me with a warm smile. "Freddi! The storm spared us both! And your friend?"

It took me a moment to realize he must have seen Lumi with me on the raft. "He is here as well. He wanted to look for, uh, food."

Ferdinand stood and gazed around

him, then back at me. "I want to thank the both of you for trying to rescue me. I can't quite fathom how I came to be here." His face grew serious and worried. "I hope my father and the others survived."

"The ship is fine, sir, as is the crew—we saw it just before we were swept away to this island. I believe if we do some searching, we may find your father and his men. I have a strong feeling they are here and fine."

He half-smiled again. "Are you a fortune teller, Freddi?"

"You know, sir, funny you should say that. Every ship has a fortune teller, and I'm one." For that matter, every great house's servants had one, too. We had to amuse ourselves during our rare moments of leisure, after all. At the Capulet house, it was one of the kitchen maids, the last person you'd expect, stout and giggly until it came time to tell us our fates, at which time she became serious as death, and nobody dared jeer at her or her proclamations. I leaned back and squinted at him appraisingly. "I think you were born under a lucky star, and this may be the luckiest day of your life. There's a reason the storm spared you, a reason you came to this island. I think you'll find that reason soon."

He looked amused, but pleasantly so. "Lucky, you say? Is there treasure on this island?"

"Treasure, yes—true treasure, more valuable than anything. A thing that cannot be bought with all the riches in the world but is worth infinitely more." I pointed into the trees where Lumi had gone. "Will you seek it now?"

He nodded and turned in that direction. "I shall certainly seek my father and the others. And if I find this treasure along the way, all the more reason to celebrate when we reunite."

Lumi

— ✳ —

I T WAS BRUTALLY hot on the island, even in the shade, and my idea of marking my path with strips of cloth torn from my vest served me doubly well. I did not worry about the impropriety of being seen so poorly dressed—we'd just survived being swept off a ship, after all. Each time I tied a strip of cloth onto a branch, I heard what could have been either leaves rustling in the wind or a soft chuckle. *Go ahead and laugh*, I thought, *just lead me to where I need to be.*

I came to the edge of a clearing in the trees, the far side of which marked a change in the terrain to a steep, rocky hill. At the base of the hill was a cave, presumably the dwelling of Prospero and Miranda, because there before the cave entrance the two stood.

Prospero appeared to be in the middle of a lengthy story, while Miranda listened attentively. I barely got a glimpse of each, however, before things suddenly changed: Miranda slumped to the ground, curled up on her side, and seemed to be sleeping. Prospero watched her for a moment, then, satisfied, gently kissed her forehead and moved to the edge of the clearing, his back to both of us.

Perplexed, I waited, then realized that whatever force or entity had been guiding me here was no longer present. At least, it was no longer in my own presence, but suddenly Prospero began to talk again, with pauses every now and then to suggest that he was having a conversation with someone—or something. I saw no one else there, but remembering Syra's tale, I figured it had to be Ariel, the airy spirit who served as Prospero's slave. Had Ariel been my guide? Had he been the storm?

Focus, Lumi. My goal was Miranda, not the other two, and I turned my attention to her.

She was wearing a dress of light blue silk (here?) in a style that had been fashionable about a decade ago, though it looked clean and new (how?) and fit her perfectly. No matter how carefully cared for, a silk dress could not have stayed that pristine for ten years on a tropical island, and there couldn't have been enough room on whatever boat brought Prospero and Miranda for things they'd need in a decade. Prospero must have magicked the dress for her, and though this was insignificant compared to the storm, it stunned me for a moment. I couldn't do that. Perhaps he'd made whatever clothes she came in, as a very young child, change and grow as she did. However he did it, that skill was beyond me.

I couldn't dawdle, though; I had to seize this opportunity while it lasted, because it was just about perfect: Miranda was sleeping and Prospero was distracted by his conversation. Quiet as a snake, I slithered through the trees around the clearing until I was right by the girl's side. Leaning close, my lips at her ear and my eyes on Prospero, I whispered, "Miranda. Please listen, Miranda. You will soon see the face of a young man. He will be a stranger to you, but he is your true love and has come for you. He shall love you all his days, and you shall love him equally."

Her head tilted slightly, as though she were indeed listening, but she did not wake. This seemed promising, but I didn't know if she had heard all that syrupy nonsense I'd babbled—or that anything would come of it even if she had.

I heard a rustling in the trees and backed away from the girl. It was Freddi and, just behind her, the prince. Freddi saw me, said something to the prince, gestured him vaguely forward, and turned around. Smart—she'd have said she wanted to go look at something, or made some excuse to be gone so the prince would be alone with Miranda. I circled back, keeping an eye on the prince, and found Freddi, who nodded and quickly hid us both from sight.

And before our eyes, the prince found Miranda.

She had awakened, rubbed her eyes in an endearingly childlike way, then sat up and stared, lips parted, immediately looking a lot less juvenile. She had seen Ferdinand, and he her. They were looking at each other the way Romeo had looked at me, and then at Juliet, and Juliet at him, the way Freddi looked when she talked about Mercutio, and the way she had just been looking at Ferdinand. It was an unmistakable look that always provoked irritation in me. These people with their cow eyes and gaping mouths as though they'd witnessed something miraculous when all they'd done was met each other's gaze. Look around enough and someone will certainly look back; what kind of miracle was that?

But in this case, I'd take the miracle, because it meant Freddi's plan was working so far.

Prospero was now looking at them too, at first surprised, then uncertain, but finally he tilted his head and muttered to the space where I assumed Ariel stood, "Ah, yes, it is happening just as I planned."

As *he* planned? Ha! He'd had nothing to do with this; it had been Freddi and me. He was astute enough to quickly glean the advantages in a match between his daughter and the prince, but the meeting had been engineered by us. I glanced at Freddi, who rolled her eyes at his words. I grinned and turned back to the scene before us.

Something hit me like a gust of wind, even though it was now completely calm. I had the very strong sensation that someone was staring at me, sharp and hard. None of the three we saw before us were looking our way and all three were engaged in their own affairs, and yet... I could feel it, coming from the direction of the empty space where Prospero had addressed Ariel.

Ariel could see us. Ariel knew we were there. And Ariel had been the mind of the storm, not Prospero.

I shook Freddi's shoulder and gestured for her to follow me away from the others. She shook her head, annoyed, and fixed her eyes back on the prince—who seemed to have forgotten Freddi completely—and Miranda. Freddi was torturing herself. I shook my head even more vehemently and pointed at the path back to the beach. She sighed and followed, leaving Prospero pretending to admonish his daughter so she'd love the boy even more. *Smart*, I thought fleetingly.

We kept walking the whole way back to the beach because I had a feeling Ariel would show himself when he was good and ready, and sure enough, the moment we stepped on the sugary sand again, a face popped into view before us, flickering like firelight, an elfin face with small, pretty features and twinkling blue eyes. The face looked us up and down appraisingly, dubiously. "And what are you?"

What, not who. Coming from a magical entity, it could have been an insult or a compliment. "I am Foschia Luminosa and this is Fiamma Fredda," I answered. "And you are Ariel."

He did not seem at all impressed that I knew who he was. "The Mist and the Flame! I am delighted to make your acquaintance. And you are the prince's guardians, are you? I saw you following him on the waters, and I saw *you*"—here he waved a delicate hand at me—"doing a bit of magic. I had to know who you were, so I brought you along to the island, and then *here*." Suddenly the face darted closer, inches away, trying to startle us. Ha, neither of us flinched. "Prospero doesn't know you're here—yet. I was merely curious. If you are no threat to my master, you need not worry."

We both remained silent for a moment. We were not a direct threat to Prospero, but he would no doubt try to make things a lot more difficult for us if he knew our purpose. Finally, cautiously, I spoke. "You made the storm."

Ariel nodded. "I was doing Prospero's bidding, but yes, that was my work."

"The storm was powerful magic. You are powerful. And yet you are enslaved?"

Ariel nodded again, approvingly. "You wish to take measure of your adversaries. That is wise. I am powerful, yes, but airy spirits cannot act on our own behalf. We need nothing— not food nor drink nor sleep—so we seek nothing but our own amusement. Prospero's magic was not equal to mine when he rescued me, but he knew the one spell that would bind me to him. Under this spell, I must bow to his will, I cannot hurt him or his daughter, and I cannot be free until he grants my release."

Now Ariel's whole body materialized, though still translucent and ever in motion like the wind. He looked elfin in body as well as visage, small and quick, dressed in a flowy tunic that rippled, sometimes azure like water and sometimes scarlet like flame. His form was admittedly pleasing to the eye, but I remained wary: this was the creature who had tormented Syra's son. "That is my story, now what is yours? Why do you protect the prince?" He darted around us, then stopped to study our faces. "But perhaps you aren't here for Prince Ferdinand. Perhaps you are here for another reason, doing someone else's bidding as I do Prospero's." He tilted his head saucily and exclaimed, "Of course! Sycorax, the witch! You're the slaves of that horrible hag."

I kept my voice and expression neutral. "Her name is Syra, and we are not her slaves. We are here by choice to help her."

Ariel laughed, a sound like a soft breeze through grasses. "By choice, are you? Tell me, did you ever think to choose not to do what she asked? What do you think would have happened if you had said no?"

Uncomfortable at these questions, I couldn't help but consider them seriously. Had we ever thought to say no? Certainly I had been skeptical—and made that clear—but I had at no point suggested I would refuse her. In fact, what had there been to refuse? She had not asked us to do this; we just... did it. An ugly thought occurred to me: were we under some kind of spell? If so, we had indeed been as good as enslaved.

Freddi interrupted my thoughts. "Syra wants us only to free her son. That's all. She said nothing about getting revenge on Prospero or anyone else. Freeing a mother's enslaved son does not seem like a terrible thing to be made to do. You, however, are being made to do terrible things. You have been told to torment the people on the island! That is very different."

Ariel's eyes glimmered like two bright stars, though it hardly seemed like cheerful twinkling—more like mischievous amusement. "Here's a challenge for you, oh Bright Mist and Cold Flame: I task you with succeeding in your mission—freeing Caliban—without doing harm to anyone else." He beamed as if he'd said something incredibly clever. "You think this a simple matter? In truth, you've already lost. You made them fall in love, and what is love without suffering?"

That made me uneasy, thinking of Romeo and Juliet and how my bringing them together almost caused their tragic deaths. Best not to think of that. "How can we have 'lost' something we never entered into in the first place? This is not meant to be a contest. We each have our tasks. I do not even see that these tasks are in direct conflict."

"Do you not? Allow me to aid your perception."

It was as if a giant hand scooped us up and held us in a tight grasp, only the hand was made of air. We were lifted, carried, and flung down again on another part of the island.

Three men sat on logs in a swampy clearing. Two were Neapolitan, one wearing the garb of a court jester and the other a bedraggled butler. The third—large, muscular, and dark, in a rough brown tunic that appeared to be fashioned from tree bark—was unquestionably Caliban. We were near enough that they could have easily spotted us, but Freddi's hiding spell must have still been working, since they never looked our way. They were passing around a bottle of wine, each guzzling loudly and sloppily when it came to him. When he didn't have the bottle, Caliban would beg the drunkest one, the butler, to be his new master. "I shall worship thee! Only do this one deed on my behalf," he beseeched pathetically. "Kill the tyrant who is my master and I shall serve you all my days!" The jester chortled and jeered, the butler gave the jester a rough shove and promptly fell over himself, and Caliban, perhaps feeling that he should not be standing when the object of his worship was lying down, dropped to the ground himself.

With a courteous bow, Ariel disappeared, leaving us staring wide-eyed and open-mouthed in dismay.

We watched the three men stumbling over rocks, slumping against trees, slurping from the bottle, and babbling all but incoherently. "So *this* is Syra's son." I couldn't keep the distaste out of my tone. A drunk who was conspiring with another drunk and a clown to commit murder—this was Syra's dear boy, who we were supposed to rescue.

"Yes. He's the one." Freddi recovered her poise quickly and frowned at me. "He's not really drunk, Lumi. It's a ruse. He's actually quite clever." At my skeptical look, she continued, "It's what you do when you're in a lowly position. You get others only slightly farther up the ladder to take action on your behalf. You make them think they're high and mighty and you get them to do what you want." She sounded very sure of herself, and I no longer felt quite so skeptical given the experiences she'd had as a servant in the House of Capulet. "He doesn't want another master. Who would? He wants to be free."

"At any cost? By committing murder?"

"Yes, at any cost. He's a slave. What else has he to lose?"

I scrutinized Caliban for several minutes. I had seen inebriated men and boys just as much as Freddi had—people at all levels of society could be drunks, after all—and Caliban's tipsiness seemed genuine. This was almost certainly the first wine he'd ever tasted, and despite his size it probably would not take much to affect him. And yet Freddi did have a point: who would choose another master over actual freedom?

"Regardless, we cannot let them kill Prospero."

"I doubt we have to worry about that. Since Ariel knows about this plot, Prospero will know, and will prevent its happening. But you can be sure they'll be punished for it as if it had happened."

Just then I saw Caliban swig from the bottle, pass it to another and, when he perceived neither of them looking his way, spit out the liquid he'd taken in. He gave the others a quick look of blazing scorn before erupting into a roar of seemingly tipsy laughter.

Before Freddi could say anything, I beat her to it. "You were right. Caliban isn't drunk. He's sober and serious. I'm not sure if that makes our job harder or easier." I thought for a moment. "No, I'm sure: it's harder. This isn't the wine talking; Caliban really wants to kill Prospero, and Prospero will never free Caliban once he knows. We'll be lucky if he lets Caliban live. How are we going to do this?"

"We could tell him his mother sent us. No," Freddi added quickly, "he wouldn't believe it. He thinks his mother is dead, and wouldn't listen to us long enough for us to prove otherwise. Anyway, I don't know that we should work on him. Caliban isn't the problem; Prospero and Ariel are."

"Caliban wants to kill Prospero. That isn't a problem?"

"That's natural and understandable. Prospero's treatment of him is neither."

I sighed and watched the three bumble off, shouting and singing and roaring with laughter. We were getting nowhere.

When we could no longer hear the trio, I studied the boggy land. "I am parched and famished," I said. "This area might be fed by fresh water from the interior. If we follow the source there might be a clearer stream to drink from."

"You study geography as well as magic?" Freddi said with amusement as we set off around the swamp.

I shrugged. "I'm interested in the world."

After a slow but short walk, we indeed found a quick-flowing stream. The waters were clear and cold, but I was so thirsty I'd probably have guzzled down the swamp water. Thirst slaked, we now looked around for something edible. A tree with peach-sized fruits drew me to it like a magnet. I picked one and examined it, though its smooth yellow skin gave me no clue as to whether it was sweet or poison. I held it to my nose and detected a faint, delicate fragrance. Surely not poisonous?

"Are you going to eat it or write poetry about it?" Freddi mumbled. I looked up and saw that she had already bitten into one of the fruits and was munching contentedly.

Unwise, I thought, but bit into the fruit myself. Inside the flesh was pink, juicy, and full of tiny, crunchy seeds—and the most delicious thing I'd ever tasted.

"Well, we won't starve, anyway," I mumbled back, my own mouth full.

"Indeed!" The exclamation was Ariel's voice, so startling I almost dropped the rest of the fruit. His face popped into view again between Freddi and me. "You have shown yourselves quite resourceful. However, I am not sure the others will fare so well. Those three sots are happy for the moment, but the King and his men have no wine to give them cheer."

I swallowed the last of the fruit and exchanged looks with Freddi. We hadn't even thought about Prospero's revenge against Duke Antonio and King Alonso, since that was only a tangent to our main concern of rescuing Caliban from slavery. "We are not part of the King's entourage and were not involved with the Duke's usurping of Prospero's title," I said carefully.

"We will only concern ourselves with them if it is in our interest or for our own protection."

"Good!" Ariel said. "Then I would be delighted to show you what is transpiring with the others. You will find it most amusing."

I saw Freddi roll her eyes, and we both braced ourselves, for we knew what would happen next. Once again, Ariel swept us away with him.

We were unceremoniously dumped back at the edge of the clearing by Prospero's cave. Miranda and Prospero were nowhere in sight, but a half-dozen large logs lay near the mouth of the cave, and Ferdinand was wearily unloading another. He straightened, sighed, and trudged back toward the trees.

"Prospero is making the lad do the same base work as the vile slave Caliban." Ariel tittered. "He must carry logs from sunup to sundown or until he drops like so much dead wood himself."

"Why?" I asked in dismay. "Does the young man not love Miranda, and would they not make an ideal match—for Prospero as well as themselves?" Had our plan backfired so miserably?

"Yes and yes, but my master is wise in all things, including matters of the heart. He would not want the prince's prize to be so easily won. And, far more important, there is of course the matter of retribution against the young man's father. After all, the crimes against my master affected his child, so why shouldn't the crimes of the King be punished through the prince?"

The fallacy of this argument rankled me, but before I could assume the appropriate lofty tones and point it out (my old tutor Grigio would have been proud, if he had been capable of it), Freddi had dashed from my side and run after the prince. I almost shouted her name but stopped abruptly when she disappeared—she'd used her own magic, I realized, to shield herself from Ferdinand.

Freddi

I GOT HIM INTO this. I could not just stand there and watch him suffer.

I matched his footsteps on the leaf-strewn path and waited until he reached a pile of timber—huge, newly fallen, and seemingly endless. I waited while he selected a log, hoisted it unsteadily, buckling visibly from the weight, and turned back toward the cave.

Before he took a step forward, I heard him whisper what sounded like a prayer: "For you, the load is but light. For you, I would do ten times this labor. For you are worth all things to me."

Unseen, I snuck up behind him and slowly (it had to be slowly—the log was immense) lifted the back of the log just as he shifted his stance. I sensed him break into a delighted smile even though I couldn't see his face.

As we moved back toward the cave, I heard him humming the Tunisian melody. I smiled too.

We made it with relative ease back

to the cave—just in time to see Prospero and Miranda returning. I relinquished the log and hastily retreated—I was not sure whether Prospero might be able to see through my magic the way Ariel had. But Prospero, seeing his daughter run to Ferdinand, swiftly backed away and vanished.

I felt a hand seize me and yank me sharply back, too—Lumi, of course, furious at me. "What do you think you're doing? Helping him, I know, but really, Freddi, you're not helping anyone by being foolhardy like that."

"Only do good," I muttered. "I didn't do that, so I was trying to undo the harm. Sound familiar?"

We were both aware that Ariel was watching us as though we were a stage play, so we ceased our quarrel and turned back to watch the scene before us.

The two young people were standing close together but chastely not touching. The prince had his hands clasped before him as he declared his love for her, while Miranda shed tears of joy. In this beautiful island setting, it would have touched the most hardened heart. It touched mine, and yet bitterness assailed me as well. It was not me, it would never be me. The prince would not know I tried to help him, nor should he (*true charity does not seek acknowledgement*, the nuns had annoyingly drilled into me for years), but what person can look at the happiness of another with unselfish joy when they have been denied that happiness themselves?

The prince knelt and asked for her hand in marriage. She most willingly agreed.

I felt Lumi's hand pulling me away again, this time gently.

Lumi

—✹—

I DID NOT KNOW what to say to Freddi. She would not want sympathy—she'd see it as pity—but I had to do something to ease her pain.

Unexpectedly, it was Ariel who took action. He said nothing to or about Freddi, instead turning to me. "Come, now! You have yet to see what has become of the others."

Again we were scooped up by the wind and carried to another part of the island, though this time we were not tossed down, at least, but set down gently. Presumably we were invisible, as the men before us did not react. Here were King Alonso and his entourage, a half-dozen men, alive and uninjured but weak from hunger and thirst. Their clothes were tattered and dirty, and if I had not seen them fleetingly on the ship I would not have known which was the King and which were his subjects, all were so equally and thoroughly brought low.

"Sorry-looking lot, aren't they," Ariel said, tutting. "Well, go on and help them, since helping people seems to be your favorite thing to do, for some incomprehensible reason." His sarcastic tone at the words "helping people" made it quite clear how he felt about it. "Here, I'll get you started."

He made a breezy gesture with an arm, and at our feet lay several loaves of fresh bread, a basket of fruit, a round of cheese, and a large jug of ale. Freddi and I eyed the veritable banquet before us, and then looked uncertainly at each other. We had only eaten a little fruit so far that day and were ourselves famished, but anything from Ariel was likely to come with a price. Would the food turn into stones the moment we bit into it? Would *we* turn into stones once we swallowed it?

"It is not poisoned or hexed or anything like that," Ariel said, seeing our hesitation. "It is real food and drink, on my honor, and it would be their salvation."

I turned to Freddi. "All right. We can say we washed ashore, too, and luckily managed to bring supplies from the ship."

"That would hardly be fair," Ariel said with a mock-pout. "They cannot see *me*, so they should not be able to see *you* either. Now what will you do?"

"You persist in pretending we are engaged in some kind of contest," I said. "We never agreed to that. As I said, we are here to help Caliban, but you prevent us from doing our task. Meanwhile, these people are suffering and you could easily help them, but you'd rather toy with them instead. Whatever is the point in that?"

"The point, my Bright Mist, is that it's amusing. I must do my master's bidding, as you must do yours, but there's no harm in enjoying ourselves along the way. My master wants them to suffer at least a *little*—and if you know his story, even as told from that old hag, you know they deserve that for their treachery."

He raised his eyebrows in mute challenge, and I had to admit, at least in my own mind, that he was right; even Syra had said that Prospero had been cheated out of his rightful title and exiled for no reason besides the jealous machinations of his brother. I said nothing, which was as much acknowledgement as Ariel needed. "And as for my 'easily helping them,' well, try it yourself. Go on, do some good." He sneered. "I'll even provide appropriate dinner music."

Ariel began to sing, or at least that was the nearest term I could use to describe the hauntingly beautiful, wordless sounds he made. His voice was sweet, the melody engaging, and rather than frightening the men, it seemed to hold them in a thrall.

"It is worth a try," Freddi whispered to me, and I nodded.

Freddi hid us both and we carried the food forward toward them, trying to move as unthreateningly as we could. The men were startled, understandably, though their eyes grew large and their mouths gaped when they saw what exactly seemed to float toward them. We set the food down and then left quickly back into the trees. Ariel had disappeared, though we could still hear his singing.

The men did not approach the victuals. Their bewilderment was stronger than their hunger. "Come on, you idiots, eat," I heard Freddi mutter. I almost laughed—Freddi charitable was not much different from Freddi adversarial.

Two of them, perhaps the hungriest—or the greediest, making sure they got their share before the others—were starting to yield. The others held firm. I tried my own magic, attempting to move them closer so that they might smell the perfume of fruit, the sharp tang of cheese.

"You cannot move them," Ariel whispered annoyingly close to my ear. "You do not have the magic to make someone do something so thoroughly against their will. They are too wary that this is a trick. And it is, but not the one they believe it to be." He tittered again.

I turned to shush him but once more he had vanished.

And then the game changed. A bright flash and the terrifying roar of thunder assailed us all. It was a sight and sound to bring the horror of the tempest back to us all. But we were not set upon by another storm. Something far more fearsome appeared: Ariel, not in the pleasing form he had shown us before but monstrous, with massive wings, sharp claws, and a face that was still definitely his but now looked—how can I describe it?—like the last thing a person might see before they perished in a grisly, violent death.

Slowly he unfurled his huge, dark wings, blotting out all sunlight, and sharply clapped them down.

The wind from his wingbeat hit Freddi and me like a punch, sending us soaring away from the others. When once again we fell to earth, we found ourselves back on the beach where we'd first landed. Whatever was happening to the King and his men at Ariel's hands—or claws—we were not to discover.

"Are you hurt?" Freddi asked.

I said no, asked the same, and received the same answer. We both lay on the sand for a while, bone tired and at a complete loss for what to do.

Still, I knew it had to be asked once again. "Freddi, how are we going to succeed? Neither of us can do anything close to that kind of magic. And Ariel was just toying with them, no doubt. If he wanted to, he could do a lot more. Who knows what he's doing even now—now that we've been removed from the scene."

"We haven't even approached Prospero yet, and we're doing

this badly against his henchman," Freddi agreed glumly. "I'm sure he knows about Caliban's plans by now. Prospero has proven himself someone who holds a grudge very hard."

"Ariel is our true foe," I reasoned, finally sitting upright but not bothering to shake off the sand. "He's Prospero's slave, too, so he ought to be on our side at least a little. He could be helping us, but he makes it a point to do the opposite. Prospero either doesn't know we're here yet because Ariel has not let him know, or else doesn't care because, as Syra said, we aren't important enough."

"Weakness," Freddi murmured, deep in thought. "We have to consider where Ariel is vulnerable, like we did for Prospero."

"You can see how well that turned out. And I don't think being a caring father could be considered a 'weakness,' either—more like something that propels him to do what's right."

"Prospero enslaved Caliban because he somehow thought it would protect Miranda," Freddi argued stubbornly. "How was *that* right?"

I could be just as stubborn. "It's still not a weakness—more like, I don't know, the key factor that could make him change his course of action."

"That's too many words. Weakness," Freddi insisted. "Caliban was enslaved and Ferdinand was saved because the one thing that would make Prospero change his plans is Miranda."

We watched a small bird darting aggressively after a larger one, chasing it down the beach. I didn't want to keep arguing so counterproductively, so I conceded, "I suppose if not for his love for his daughter—and his daughter's love for Ferdinand—Prospero might have tortured the prince to get back at King Alonso. He still made the poor boy carry those ridiculous logs all day, though."

Freddi bit her lip, and I wished I hadn't brought up Ferdinand's toil, as it was obviously still a sore spot for her, probably both emotionally and physically. Those logs were enormous. "He would have done worse otherwise. The point is Miranda is his vulnerability, or whatever you want to call it. What is Ariel's? What is *he*, for that matter?"

"He's proud. He's curious," I listed.

"He's a trickster," Freddi offered.

"He likes being entertained."

"He likes *you*."

"What?" I glared at Freddi, but she was not teasing. Her expression was serious.

"He *likes* you. Or at least he seems interested in you. I don't mean the way a human boy would be—Ariel would hardly be interested in your body since he barely has a solid one himself. But he seems to be paying an awful lot of attention to us, and mostly to you. Why, when we should be as unimportant to him as we are to Prospero?"

I hardly knew what to think about any of that. "Well, however 'interested' he is in me, it's not enough to constitute a weakness."

Freddi shrugged. "No, I suppose not. If anything, this might be making it worse for us—he won't leave us alone." She chewed her lip. "What else? Obviously he's powerful—"

"—but enslaved." I sighed. "And only Prospero can free him. So we can't use that as threat or enticement either way. If only we could…"

"Yes?" Freddi asked, eager and impatient.

I took a deep breath, smelled the complex, entwined fragrances of the island, and exhaled slowly. "I have an idea, but I cannot tell it to you. Seriously, Freddi, I can't, or it might not work. I'm not trying to be mysterious and dramatic. You'll know what I'm doing when the time comes."

Freddi stared at me for a moment and then shrugged. "All right."

That was all she said. It amazed me how far we'd come—my cousin actually trusted me. That was good, because I wasn't even sure I trusted myself in this idea.

I stood and lifted my head. "Ariel," I said aloud. "You know why we're here. If you want this fight, or contest, or whatever you want to call it—if you want it to be fair, you'll cease dragging us around the island and let us go to Caliban."

After only a few seconds, a funnel of sand blew up from the beach. When it settled, Ariel was there, back in his original, wingless form. "Yes, Bright Mist, you will definitely want to go to Caliban right away. I suppose you would refuse my help in bringing you to him, though in the interest of fairness I am at your service." He gave a low, graceful bow, but then raised his head with a sly smirk. "You probably should accept. Prospero is not in a very forgiving mood at the moment."

I glanced at Freddi. It might take hours for us to locate Caliban on our own, which of course Ariel already knew. Freddi nodded, without enthusiasm, so I said to Ariel, "Very well. Take us to Caliban."

As Ariel swept us away, I thought grimly, *We are not in a forgiving mood either.*

⚬

If they had looked pathetic before, now Caliban and the other two resembled doomed souls wandering the depths of hell. They were filthy from head to toe, and blood trickled from multiple scratches on their arms and legs. The King's men, still inebriated, were squabbling with each other about some non-sense or other, but Caliban, sober now as before, darted wary looks around him, urging the others to be quiet with frantic gestures.

"The assassination plot is not quite proceeding according to plan," Ariel whispered.

"What have you done to them?" Freddi asked, her own whisper harsh with fury.

"That matters a lot less than what will yet be done to them," was Ariel's malicious answer. "To be sporting, I will give you a little time to prepare."

He waved an arm. Distantly we heard the baying of what sounded like hunting hounds, which, as the sound came rapidly closer, turned into fierce snarls. Caliban froze just as Freddi and I did, all three of us mirrors of terror.

"They can't be real," I said

"The food was real," Freddi said.

We stared at each other, and then we saw the dogs. Those teeth sure looked real.

Caliban shrieked, yanking the other two up and away. The dogs tore after them, four enormous beasts snapping their jaws at their intended victims. Freddi grabbed my arm. "We need to draw them away!"

Disguised by Freddi's magic, we raced after the dogs, yelling and thrashing at tree branches to get their attention. It was a plan of desperation—if the dogs were real, we were in just as much danger as the others were, for even invisible we could be detected by our smell.

Two of the hounds continued after Caliban's group, while two of them peeled off and turned toward us. They growled, all raised hackles and bared teeth. The fact that they couldn't see us had not diminished their ferocity. Freddi grabbed a stout branch from the ground and held it before her like a sword, motioning me to get behind her. Remembering old Bruno, I tried to focus on locking minds with the dogs, hoping to calm them. For a moment we all stood there locked in place, Freddi ready to battle, the dogs ready to pounce, and I trying to think happy canine thoughts about napping in the sun.

We'll never know what did it—the dogs' uncertainty, Freddi's branch-brandishing, my mind lock, or possibly (much as I hated to consider it) Ariel's own interference—but the dogs as one closed their mouths, wagged their tails, and lay down.

Two very large sighs escaped us, then we heard anguished cries somewhere in the distance. "I'd love to pet you, pups, but we have your buddies to deal with now," I said soothingly, and Freddi and I were off again.

Following the cries, we found Caliban leaning against a rock, several bloody marks on his leg. He'd been mauled, and though the wounds were not deep, he clenched his fists in pain. The other two men and dogs were nowhere to be seen.

"Oh Father, oh Mother, help me, help!" Caliban moaned.

We ran to him, and Freddi put her hands against his leg to stop the bleeding. Caliban shrieked at her touch. "What, more of Prospero's devils come to torment me? Show yourselves or begone!"

It occurred to both of us simultaneously that Ariel, who had insisted we not be seen when we tried to present the King and his men with food, must have been keeping us invisible now as well. I was beyond angry with that wicked spirit, but I calmed myself as quickly as I could and locked my mind with Caliban's.

My son, it is I, Sycorax. Listen to me: the dogs are not real. The pain is not real. This is more of Prospero's trickery. Ignore it. Listen instead to the island, to its music. The pain will go away and you will be healed.

Gradually Caliban stopped thrashing and writhing. His body relaxed, his countenance became peaceful, and he leaned against the rock in an exhausted slump.

Freddi tugged at my sleeve. "I think the wound is not too bad," she whispered. "I don't know what you did but it worked—nicely done. Perhaps we should leave him here to rest."

I nodded, and we backed silently away.

Ariel appeared then, with his usual amused smirk. "Wasn't that fun? Only think," he purred, "what Prospero might do to *you* when he finds out you work for Sycorax."

I stared hard at him, that elfin face with its delicate features, that light and airy form hovering before us, and I knew what I had to do.

"Stop, Ariel," I said quietly. "You win." Freddi shot me an alarmed look, which I ignored. "You've beaten us, because no, we cannot do what we want without harming anyone. Harm must come."

I was ready. I closed my eyes and let it happen: my legs shredding into thin strands, sinking into the earth, my torso thickening, my skin becoming rough and hard. Hundreds, then thousands, of green needles began poking through the skin of my arms, neck, and face. My blood became thick, its flow slowing. My heart was a knot of wood.

The last thing I heard was a wailing, a keening, a shriek: Ariel, sharing my thoughts, sharing the sensations I felt, as we both became encased in bark, rooted to the ground, reaching for sunlight, two more among the many trees of the island.

Freddi

"COUSIN! COUSIN, DO you hear me? Please, Lumi."

She stood statue-still, eyes closed, a mirror of Ariel. It took me a moment to realize, albeit dimly, what had happened: she had made Ariel believe she magicked him back into becoming a tree. At the same time—or perhaps the only way she could do so—she had convinced herself that she was making the same transformation. While it had worked to immobilize Ariel, I knew I desperately needed to stop the spell, and fast: trees don't breathe the way people do.

"Think, Lumi. Think about your life. It's a human life. Do you remember when we first met? I do—I'll never forget the look on your face when I told you who I was. Here's something I didn't tell you, though, that I realized at that moment: you were the first family member I had ever met, had ever talked to—the only family I have, and probably the only friend as well. Do you remember?"

She was barely breathing, her heart a weak, slow flutter, her skin cool as leaves.

"Do you remember," I whispered fervently again, and her eyelids flickered once, twice. Her lips twitched. She whispered, "Yes, I remember."

Then her eyes flew open. She panted as if she'd been running. "Did I do it?" she gasped.

I blinked several times and realized I had to let her believe she'd really worked some kind of shape-changing spell; otherwise, Ariel might realize what had happened and know that she didn't really have such powers. "Yes, Lumi. You did it."

Out of the corner of my eye, I saw Ariel also begin moving again. He whirled around several times, as if he needed to shake himself free of the feeling of entrapment. He darted a look at Lumi. "Cruel," he muttered, and I detected a note of admiration in his voice.

She quickly stood and faced him, keeping her expression neutral. Ariel had a similar look, and I guessed that both of them were trying not to show just how shaken they were by the experience. "You say I've won," Ariel finally spoke, "because you could not win without causing harm. And, brilliantly, you also have won: the harm you've done has made its point. I will do my best to convince Prospero to cease tormenting Caliban and the others."

"And to free him," I interjected.

He gave me a cold look. "I am not free yet myself."

"He will listen to you, though," Lumi said quietly. "There is no one else he confers with, no one else he trusts, as much as you."

I had to marvel at Lumi. Despite the recent trauma, she had gathered her wits quickly and had chosen just the right bit of flattery to appease Ariel—and she backed it with the solid threat that she knew what scared Ariel the most.

The combination worked. Ariel nodded his elfin head and vanished.

Lumi

— ✦ —

WE WERE BACK at the cave. Either Ariel had somehow managed to do what we asked and convinced
Prospero to forgive his enemies, or the great magician had come to that point on his own, but regardless, Ariel
had returned us to this place with the assurance that we need no
longer be hidden.

As we entered the clearing, we saw Ferdinand and Miranda
seated in front of the cave on two stumps, with a larger stump
between them. They were playing chess—the game he'd talked
about playing with Freddi. It was sweet, the two of them happy
in each other's presence, making quiet small talk about various
moves and strategies, enjoying the moment together. I knew
what a painful thing it had to be for Freddi to witness.

All she said was, "It worked. Our plan worked. Look at
them." She herself, however, looked away.

Ferdinand saw Freddi and leapt off his stump to greet
her. "Good Freddi! Your fortune telling talents deserve
the highest praise—you were right!

I did find a truly great treasure," he said, gesturing toward Miranda.

Freddi nodded toward the girl, who ran over as well. "Freddi and Lumi!" she exclaimed with delight.

I froze and stared, panicked, at Freddi. How did Miranda know *my* name? The girl smiled charmingly and said, "My father told me who you are. He said you are apprentice sorcerers retained by a friend of King Alonso to protect him and Prince Ferdinand."

Did he now? That must have been Ariel's doing, I reasoned, so that we could finally show ourselves and (I hoped) return with the others to Naples.

"For which," Miranda continued, gazing fondly at the prince, "I owe you my deepest gratitude."

"I as well," said Ferdinand. "Also, my apologies," he said to Freddi, "if I acted in any way improperly while you were disguised as a sailor. I did not know the truth, of course."

Nor would he ever, I thought sadly, for while this had a modicum of truth, it still didn't even scratch the surface of Freddi's real story. Freddi bowed stiffly, uncomfortable with both the thanks and the apology. An awkward moment passed before a rustling in the trees announced the arrival of the others—King Alonso, his men, and finally Prospero, who nodded briefly in our direction before turning toward his daughter.

"Well, that was anticlimactic," I muttered to Freddi. "All our talk about taking on Prospero, and it's over before we started."

She tried to snort derisively, but it came out sounding more like a sigh. Ahead of us, surrounded by the others, Miranda exclaimed "Oh wonder!" as she beheld them, her sweet innocence ringing through the trees.

Miranda

FERDINAND BOTH WAS and wasn't my first love.
It is difficult to explain something I don't half understand myself. I remember saying that exact same thing to Cal once and hearing him repeat back only a part: *You don't half understand yourself.* He was right, whether he meant it that way or not. I think most people don't half understand themselves but they decide *this is who I am* to make things easier—so that they can believe they fully understand. That is, if they're lucky they get to decide. For others, it's decided for them.

My father decided everything for me. I owed him my life several times over; it was the least I could do in return. There was only one thing I ever decided for myself, though at the time I didn't realize it was any kind of choice. It just happened: I loved Caliban, and he loved me.

He was my brother, my best friend, my only friend. He was my Cal and I was his Mia. Sometimes it seemed we were each other, two parts of the same person. My father was busy with his studies, and anyway he was my *father*; he could never be anything else. I did my chores and my studies and all the things I needed to do to please him, but that still left me much of the day to myself, when he sent me off because the work he was doing was difficult and dangerous and he must not be interrupted or distracted. So I went off to play with Cal. We climbed trees, picked their nuts and fruits, and leapt off into space from the top branches. We caught small monkeys and birds, made friends with them and let them go with a wave goodbye. We splashed under waterfalls, hid in caves, cartwheeled down the beach until we collapsed screaming with laughter in sand-crusted heaps. Father didn't care at first; he said I was a good girl, his pride and joy, and perhaps some of my goodness would benefit *that boy*. That was how he saw our relationship, so as we grew up together, that was what we allowed him to see.

And grow up we did.

Caliban didn't speak my language—he didn't speak any language I had ever heard before. Instead, he sang the wordless tunes of the island, and the island accompanied him. Birds, breeze-blown grasses and leaves, waves rolling back and forth across the sand all joined in a complex and wonderful harmony. I learned to sing that way too, so we could all communicate together. And then our songs started to change, because we were changing. It was exciting—and scary. I was not afraid of Cal, though, only my father.

Caliban had always wanted to teach me about the island he loved so much; I taught him my language so that he could do just that. This worked perfectly as a way we could be together without my father suspecting anything else might happen. I was merely teaching him to speak; he was merely an ignorant savage who needed to be civilized. Things were different after that. The more language I taught him, the less inclined he was to reciprocate with his own lessons. "I cannot talk about this place with your words" was how he put it. Something else changed, too: we were no longer friends delighting in the world around us, exploring it together. I was his teacher. I corrected his mistakes. He resented my corrections and deliberately made more mistakes. I scolded. He refused to learn more. He said I sounded more like my father every day. I said, "And you sound more like the way he thinks of you: a savage beast."

Then it was over. We became the things we accused each other of, the things we were only going to pretend to be so that our real selves would not be discovered by my father. In his presence we each said the unforgivable thing:

"I should have raped you when I had the chance."

"You'll never be more than a savage brute and you deserve to be enslaved."

And so my father saw us hate each other without ever knowing we'd been in love.

When the spirit whispered in my dream that the next young man I saw would be my true love, I thought Cal would be there—who else? Even the part about his being a stranger made sense to me, as he and I had become strangers to each other. I half feared and half hoped it would be Cal. But it wasn't. Can you imagine my wonder upon beholding Ferdinand? I had seen no other beings that I remembered in my life other than my father and Caliban. Of course I thought the prince a splendid miracle. Of course I loved him. And so I ended up with someone my father would have wanted for me rather than the person I'd wanted for myself.

Was it a betrayal? Of all the things Cal said to me, he never said that. A betrayal is a surprise. Perhaps his father's warning about *those people, the people who are coming* meant that he'd expected it all along. I was one of *them*, and I could not be trusted. All the terrible things my father did to him still did not surprise him in the least. In that way, he kept his dignity, his pride.

And then the others came. They were everything Cal had feared, everything his father had warned him about: the men, pale as death, coming to take the island from him. And yet here was the mightiest of them, a King, kneeling, in tears, before two children, begging forgiveness of them. They were not all evil, not any more than Cal was. They were powerful, without question; if they wanted his land, there was little he or I, lacking power, could do. But wasn't peace still possible? Could they not be kind and merciful, as Ferdinand's dear father was being, as well as powerful?

"How many goodly creatures are there here! How beauteous mankind is!"

My father thought it was naivete that made me speak thus. It was not. I said it for Cal, in case he should be listening. I said it in hopes that he might see we weren't all monsters. But I also said it for myself, hoping with all my heart it might be true.

Lumi

---※---

NO SOONER HAD all the island's inhabitants gathered when one of the King's men announced that their ship, intact, the men unharmed, was waiting in the harbor to take us back to Naples. There wasn't much time left, and I still had one important task.

Just before the announcement was made, Syra had spoken to me—magically, of course. Her voice was as clear as if she were standing right before me, yet no one else could hear.

I want you to tell my son this. He is free. He knows that because he's been told that, but he may not know entirely what that means. His freedom extends beyond the confines of that island. He can see the world, like his father did, if that is his wish; he can go find his father's people, should he choose; and—he can come to see me. That is the only way he will find out about me, because I promised his father I would never seek him out myself. Caliban has the freedom to decide, but he should understand that the choices are not easy. The world is a hard place, full of evil. His father's people may reject him, since he is not like them—this is why his father did not go with them those years ago, though he would not tell Caliban that. And as for me—well, for him to come to me would mean he forgives me, and I can't ever expect that of him.

"Syra—do you want me to convince him to see you?" I said aloud. Freddi, standing next to me, raised her eyebrows.

Convince—no. Give him the option. He can decide for himself.

But of course she wouldn't have given that option if she didn't really want it.

So as we all gathered on the beach to part, I boldly approached the sullen Caliban and spoke. "Caliban, we—Freddi and I—would like to offer you our service in a matter that concerns you."

"Your service? Ha!" he spat. He addressed not just me and Freddi but everyone there. "I know better than to believe an offer such as that. You seek gratitude for your good deeds in freeing me, is that it? Oh, yes, I am grateful—that you all are leaving. You cannot steal something, then return it and expect to receive thanks."

I was taken aback. Freddi and I had not been the ones to take anything from him, and we were not seeking his gratitude, but all that was beside the point. "I ask not for thanks. I merely note that you are free, and in light of this freedom you may go anywhere you like, and that includes the land of your mother. And if you do want that, we can assist you. But it is your choice. You are no longer constrained by anyone."

"This place has never constrained me. This is my *home*. It has always been my home even when you all tried to take it from me. It was *never* yours. That is something you cannot understand, and I pity you for it." Again he seemed to be speaking to everyone present—and, peculiarly, I thought, to Miranda, who looked down and then away, eyes tracing the shoreline border between the land and the sea. I supposed it was because she, like he, had grown up here, that of all of them she might also have the right to call this her home, since she'd known no other. But he was pointedly excluding her from that now, and she—well, what could she say? A new home awaited her with her husband.

Now Caliban threw his arms wide, gesturing at the natural splendor around him. "This is my home. It will always be my home. Even after I'm dead, I'll belong to it. I'll be buried here—I'll be part of it forever! I pity anyone who doesn't have what I have."

With that he smiled proudly, turned his back on us, and walked away toward the heart of the island.

⋊

He was replaced in an instant by Ariel, who appeared before me just as the others began moving up the gangplank to the waiting ship.

"Foschia Luminosa. I thank you for a most enthralling series of events."

"Delighted you enjoyed them," I said dryly, then with more sincerity, "I thank you for 'explaining' our presence on the island. If you had not, I am not sure how Freddi and I would have been able to leave."

He waved the thanks away. "Easily done. I could not have lied to Prospero while I was still his slave, but once he freed me—well, a harmless little untruth surely is no crime?"

His playful expression changed and he became more serious—or at least as serious as must have been possible for him.

"And I am, in fact, free. Unlike that creature Caliban, I am not bound here on this island—I had only been passing by on my way elsewhere when I decided to stop and explore. I've now *thoroughly* explored it and I'm ready to move on. Won't you join me?"

Because of what Freddi had said about Ariel's interest in me, the question was not a complete shock. Still, I struggled to keep my countenance steady. A half-smirk was already twitching Ariel's lips. "Oh you needn't worry about your virtue or whatever it is your kind is always worried about. I am not concerned with matters of the flesh." His lip curled in disgust, though I suspected it was mainly for show, because he immediately added, "I think we would be good companions as we journey the world. That is what you want, isn't it?"

It was indeed, but still I could not give a direct answer. "I can't imagine how that would work. I'm not like you; I can't just fly around everywhere as I please. I must be concerned with matters of *my* flesh."

He waved a hand. "You already know I can take care of those kinds of concerns easily. I can fly us both wherever we want. I can provide you all necessary sustenance. These are but trifles, easily accomplished."

I did know, and that was one of the things bothering me. "Ariel—you admire Prospero, don't you?"

Surprised by the question, Ariel nevertheless nodded his head. "I do. He is brilliant."

"At times, even enslaved by him, you enjoyed his company?" Again, Ariel nodded, but also frowned, like he could already see where this was going. "And yet, you still had to do what *he* wanted, because he had power over you. No matter how much regard you had for him, he was still your master, and he required your subservience alone. Your esteem for him—and his for you—was irrelevant."

"Foschia Luminosa," he said with a wry look, "you would *not* be my slave."

"Nor could I ever be your equal," I said gently. "You would decide where we went and you would control how we got there. I would be grateful, I would admire you, but you would still have a certain power over me. That's not what I want, and I know you can understand that."

Ariel bowed gallantly. If he was disappointed, I could not discern it from his expression, which was merry and mischievous as ever. But just before he vanished, he waved his arms, and a mist, sparkling like sun on water, surrounded us both for an instant before he puffed his breath and blew it away. Then he disappeared, all but his voice: *I will see you again, Bright Mist.*

We were silent for a long time on the ship back to Italy. I felt many things: sad for Syra, who would never see her son; relieved and yet wistful that our adventure on the island was over; confused about Ariel, irritated about Ariel, a number of other unsettled things about Ariel.

Freddi had been brooding over something I knew she wanted to tell me, so I waited patiently and let her decide when or whether to say it. Finally, after an excellent breakfast in our quarters—yes, we now had actual quarters, not crates, and good ones, courtesy of Prince Ferdinand and Princess Miranda—Freddi pushed aside her plate and spoke.

"It didn't work. Or at least not the way you think it did. The spell, I mean, the one that was supposed to make Ariel a tree."

I said nothing for a moment, to see if she wanted to add anything. She did, hastily saying, "The result was the same—we won. You thought it worked, so Ariel did too."

I nodded. "I got the idea from something Friar Lawrence told me the very first time I tried magic. He said it was dangerous to use magic to make someone believe something that wasn't true because the only way it would work would be if I believed it as well. I knew I could access Ariel's tree memory, but with the mind lock I couldn't just make him think it was happening again against his will. And since I'd be able to see that he wasn't actually transforming, I had to experience it myself. So I told myself, *Just try it. Imagine you really can do this.*" I laughed. "It's how I worked the very first magic I did on Romeo—just gave it a try, and somehow it worked." I closed my eyes for a moment. "It did feel incredibly real at the time."

"Well, of course. It was brilliant—Ariel believed it too."

I moved to the window to stare out at the endless blue-gray water, mirror-calm but deep with mystery. "It *was* rather cruel to do that to him. He thought he was going to be a pine tree again, the worst thing I could have done to him." I chuckled. "I rather enjoyed it—being a tree, I mean, not making him one. I've always wanted to know how trees see the world." Freddi raised an eyebrow. "All right, I also enjoyed *that*. Making *him* suffer for a change. But that means Ariel was right. You can't do anything truly out of kindness, without any harmful repercussions."

"Well, why bother doing anything at all then," Freddi snorted. "Why learn magic, why learn anything, why go on adventures and explore the world. Someone's just going to get hurt."

"You know it's more complicated than that, Cousin."

"Speaking of adventures and exploring the world," she said, filling my water glass and looking like she was trying very hard to be casual, "did you really not for one moment consider going with Ariel?"

I sighed. "I was—tempted," I confessed. "Very tempted. In some ways, he was offering me what I'd always wanted."

She sipped from her own glass. "Are you going to regret not going?"

The question surprised me—I'd thought for sure she was going to ask why I said no. "I don't think so. So far I've had no regrets about anything I've done since going to La Fortezza, in spite of everything. And there's been a *lot* of everything."

Freddi joined me at the window and after a moment spoke again. "Lumi, haven't you ever wondered why Prospero never went after us?"

She was full of surprise questions this morning. "We weren't important," I stammered. "Isn't that what Syra had said would be the case? Doesn't that make sense?"

"Frankly, no, it doesn't. We *were* important. We changed things. We got Ferdinand and Miranda together, and we saved Caliban. Maybe those things would have happened anyway, but I don't think Prospero, in his paranoia, would have just shrugged off two unexpected additions to the island, especially ones that could do a little magic."

"But he didn't know we had abilities in magic."

"Yes, and *why was that*?" To my blank look, Freddi gave me a little shake of the shoulders. "Lumi, Ariel was protecting us. Prospero didn't even know we existed until after he'd ceased seeking revenge against his enemies. That's Ariel's doing, because if not for Ariel, Prospero most certainly would have considered us enemies as well!"

I stared at her, open-mouthed and flabbergasted. "No. That can't be. Freddi, he—Ariel is amoral. He didn't torment those people merely because he had no choice—he enjoyed it. Even before Prospero enslaved him, he taunted and teased Caliban. You think I'd trust someone like that?"

"Of course not. I wouldn't trust that breezy bastard either," she said, slipping into her mariner's voice, and we both guffawed. "However," Freddi continued, gazing out over the water, "that doesn't mean he's completely incapable of an occasional act of kindness. Whether you—and he—like it or not, he *did* care enough to save you from Prospero's wrath."

I sighed. "I don't want to think about Ariel anymore—not because it might make me regret anything but because I want to put all that behind me and go back home."

"Hmm," Freddi murmured. "Home. I've been thinking about what Caliban said. He would be thrilled to know that I do envy him. He has a home that he loves, that loves him back now that it belongs solely to him. That's something I daresay neither of us has."

I had not thought of this before. Freddi was right; she could not claim any particular place or people as hers, and as for me, I had abandoned my home, given it up, just like that, and while I didn't regret it now, perhaps one day I would. But that was another thing I didn't want to dwell on at the moment. "No, we may never have that. We just have—the rest of the world."

"I'm sorry you didn't get to see Tunis at all," Freddi said.

I shrugged. "Tunis is still there. We can always go back. We can go anywhere now."

"Where would you like to go?"

I thought for a moment. *Everywhere* was the answer that first came to mind. I shot a mental arrow at an imaginary map and looked to see where it landed. "How does Denmark sound to you?"

"Cold."

I grinned. "So, perfect, in other words. You're the Cold Flame, after all."

She grinned as well. "And you're the Bright Mist, Cousin. Denmark it is."

ACKNOWLEDGMENTS

I give tremendous thanks to my publisher, Mary Maddox, who makes my writerly aspirations reality while being a great writer herself—and a great friend.

Huge thanks also go to my wonderful editor, Alexandra Paterson, for her all her work to help the course of this novel run smooth.

Thanks as well to Cynthia Boatright Raleigh, Rob Hall, and Emily Still for their astute suggestions and guidance along the way.

To Shan-Ying, Leonard, and Laura, for a lifetime of support— my deepest gratitude.

And to Ken, for being with me for the long run.